DIN

ROTHERHAM LIBRARY & INFORMATION SERVICE

R7G1

This book must be returned by the date specified at the time of issue as
the DATE DUE FOR RETURN.
The loan may be extended (personally, by post, telephone or online) for
a further period if the book is not required by another reader, by quoting
the above number / author / title.

Enquiries: 01709 336774

www.rotherham.gov.uk/libraries

BLIND CAÑON

A Western Duo

Will Henry

CHIVERS

British Library Cataloguing in Publication Data available

This Large Print edition published by AudioGO Ltd, Bath,
2013.
Published by arrangement with Golden West Literary
Agency

U.K. Hardcover   ISBN   978 1 4713 2654 7
U.K. Softcover   ISBN   978 1 4713 2655 4

Printed and bound in Great Britain by
TJ International Limited

TABLE OF CONTENTS

5

Bandits of
Tehuantltux

I

"Gomez," inquired Pato, "why don't you come along with us and be bandits?"

Gomez swabbed the bar top. He studied the fly resting on the considerable bulb of his nose.

"Me," he said, "a bandit?"

"Why not? Among the three of us, we have it all. I supply the quality. Perro brings his dog-like devotion. And you, Gomez . . . ah, you have the. . . ."

"I have the gun," interrupted the proprietor of the Golondrina. "You do not fool me, Pato. I am a shrewd man."

"Exactamente," surrendered the other.

"And I own this *cantina,* also," declared Gomez.

"Of course. A man of property as well as of craft."

From the darkest corner of the earthen-floored room, the slow-minded youth who was called Perro nodded earnestly.

"A true thing, *compañeros!*" he called. "Very true."

Pato ignored him, watching Gomez. "Look, *patrón,*" he said, "come with me to the door here, *por favor.*"

Gomez laid aside his sour bar rag. He did not, however, disturb the fly on his nose. The small creature was known to him and not a bad fellow, either.

At the door he squinted his eyes at the bright sunlight. "Well," he said to Pato, "which way will you have me look?"

"At the river," directed the other. "What do you see?"

"Water," answered Gomez.

"Very good. What else?"

"Sand."

"Also good. What else?"

"A small city on the other side of the channel."

"Excellent. Do you recognize this small city?"

"Most certainly. I was born there. That is Tehuantltux. I once owned a fine *cantina* in that city."

"Yes, and what of the fine *cantina?* Where is it now?"

"Why, it is here, where we stand in it, on this side of the river, where it has been ever since the big flood."

"Precisely, *patrón.* Now what else do you see of Tehuantltux on this side of the river, other than your fine *cantina?*"

"Sand and water, that is all."

"And the good blue sky, eh, Gomez? All the rest is gone with the flood. The *cantina* is cut off from Tehuantltux, no? Do I say a true thing?"

At this, Perro, the giant boy with the mind of the newest baby, bobbed his shaggy head and cried out: "A true thing, *compañeros!* Very true."

The mindless youth had trotted up from his dark corner in the *cantina* to join them in the sunlight of the open doorway. Pato who had found him abandoned to die in a Tehuantltux trash can as a newborn child and had reared and trained him precisely as any kind-hearted wayfarer would rear and train the orphaned stray of such an origin — as a servant, a companion, a faithful pet — Pato now gave Perro a kindly pat on the head. "Go back into your corner and lie down," he said. And Perro, far larger than any man in Tehuantltux even if but fourteen years of age, barked obediently and trotted back into the *cantina.* Turning around three times, he lay down under his table, the last one in the corner, and, ever dog-like, began to pant contentedly.

11

"He is a good fellow," said Pato. "Now, then, Gomez, do we agree I speak the truth? There has not been one human customer in the Golondrina since the flood washed away the bridge?"

"You have been in it," pointed out Gomez.

"I am not a customer. I am a friend."

"Well, Perro, then."

"Perro is scarcely human, much less a customer."

"He drinks my wine."

"But he does not pay for it. Does a dog offer money for the water in the gutter of the street?"

"You call my place a gutter?"

"Never. I only say that Perro does not pay."

"Perro is poor. He has no money. Why should he pay?"

"If he has no money, why should you give him wine?"

"He is my friend."

"And what am I?"

"You are my friend, too, Pato. You don't pay me for the wine, either."

"Bah, you're impossible!"

"*Sí,* but I have the gun, eh?"

"The gun?"

"Yes, to be bandits with."

12

"Oh, of course, that gun. All right, now, shut up. No more fooling, Gomez. Do you want to go with us and be bandits, or don't you? Forget the gun."

Gomez went back to his bar. He began slapping the sour rag against the dark wet wood. The fly got up and buzzed away from its rest on his nose. There was a displeased vibrancy to its departure. Gomez took alarm.

"A thousand pardons, Guillermo!" he called out after the fly. "Come back. I have something for you." He reached beneath the bar, and brought forth a moldy piece of cheddar, a very ancient, very important wedge of cheese. "Have a bit of the best, *amigo*," he added apologetically. "It's from the interior. Made from the milk of mountain cattle."

The fly wheeled about, banking sharply in its flight. It returned, settled upon the cheese, fell to feeding greedily.

"Remarkable," observed Pato. "Consider the order of its intelligence. The brain must be no larger than the egg of a flea, yet it hears you and responds. You are a gifted man, *jefe.* And you thought I sought after you only for the gun!"

A glow, almost, suffused the round, sweat-beaded face of Porfirio Gomez.

"Jefe." He sighed. "You call me that, Pato? Your leader?"

"Forgive it, old friend," pleaded the other. "It slipped out. It is the natural way in which you take command, in which you issue an order. Why, that fly turned about as though it had been sent for by Zapata or Juárez, even Villa, perhaps. I don't see how you do it, Porfirio."

"*De nada.* It's really nothing, Pato. You know my grandfather was with Santa Anna at the Alamo. A *coronel* of the cavalry. It is in the blood."

"The Alamo, you say? I always thought your grandfather was at Goliad."

"What? My grandfather at Goliad? Never. Only cowards were there. We lost, didn't we?"

"But brave men sometimes lose, Gomez. That's a fact.

"No, no, you don't trick me. My grandfather was at the Alamo, where we won."

"If you say so." Pato could be gracious. "How about being bandits with us, *Coronel?* It is all the more important to have you as our leader now. I hadn't known about the grandfather at the Alamo. All the time I thought he was at Goliad. *¿Qué tal?*"

Gomez glowed a bit more. This idea of being bandits had its attractions. The

14

Golondrina was a splendid *cantina,* but it would never make another *peso* so long as the river had split it away from the town of Tehuantltux and no move was made to rebuild the bridge that Pato had said lay now upon the beach at Escopal. But out-lawry had its risks, too.

"I don't know." He was worried. "Killing people and taking their money can be hard work. Sometimes they object to being robbed or shot. Even a *pistolero* must take care."

"Man must work," said Pato sternly. "God put him here to toil. Besides, a danger exists in all callings. Moreover, a good bandit does much for the community. He takes from the rich and gives to the poor. Mother Church welcomes him. He prays little and lies at confession but puts much gold in the plate when it is passed. Women also seek after him. He is kind to little children. Dogs love him. I would not want to say that being bandits is all hard work, *amigo.* One must think of the other benefits as well."

Gomez licked his lips. "Where are you going to be bandits?" he asked.

"Up there." Pato flung a lank arm toward the interior plateau. "On the high plain, out of this rotten jungle swamp and desert of hot sand where we dwell. Up in that good

15

clean air, that's where all the *bandidos* are, and all of the horses, and the gold, and the women."

"Ah, those women!" breathed Gomez. *"!Santisima!"*

"You will do it, then, Porfirio? You will go with us?"

"Well, I don't know, Pato."

"*Jefe,* we need you. You are the *pistolero.* The leader. The chief. What are Perro and Pato without you?"

"Hungry," said Gomez.

"What?" Pato was stunned. "You begrudge us the food we accept from you? For shame!"

Gomez spread his pudgy hands. "No, no, it is not that I resent feeding you these twelve years, Pato," he said. "In truth, what would the Golondrina have been without you and Perro and all of those tricks you have taught him to do and which he performs better than any real dog? Such as fetching the thrown stick, sitting up and begging, rolling over and playing dead, jumping through the hoop. All of these things have been very good for business. I would never say you two old comrades had not earned your food. My idea was solely that. But for Gomez, you both would have starved."

Pato, hard against the merciless viewpoint of the *capitalista,* surrendered. "Exactly my position," he explained. "If you don't go with us to be bandits, we will die of cold and hunger upon some lonely mountain road up there. But with Gomez the bandit to lead us . . . ah, the gold, the women, the rich life!"

"Gomez the bandit," muttered the proprietor of the Golondrina. "It does have a ring to it."

"But not enough of a ring, *jefe.* Try *El Tigre.*"

"Me?" The voice of Porfirio Gomez grew weak with emotion. "Do you mean that I shall be *El Tigre?*"

"Why not? Don't you like the sound of the Tiger of Tehuantltux?"

"The Tiger of Tehuantltux," breathed Gomez.

"There is a condition," warned Pato. "Perro and myself, we shall call you merely Tiger. But that is strictly as a privilege of old friends."

"I would insist on it." The Tiger of Tehuantltux blushed.

"Glory to God," announced Pato, raising his arms as he had seen the *padre* do on somber occasions. "Bless this fearless leader and his humble followers, oh, Father. Guide us on our mission of mercy to relieve the poor. In the name of the Father, the Son, and the Holy Goat, Amen."

"Ghost! Ghost!" cried Gomez in alarm. "The Holy Ghost!"

"Ghost, Goat, what's the difference?" demanded Pato. "Religion is like love. It is in the heart of the individual."

From the gloom beyond the reach of the oil lamp on the bar, the flat-toned voice of the third of the bandits of Tehuantltux echoed its high refrain. "A true thing, *compañeros,* very true."

"You see?" said Pato to Gomez. "Even Perro understands the nobility of your commitment, *jefe.*" Then, before Gomez might deny the connection, he began to whistle and clap his hands and call out excitedly. "*Hai,* Perro! Come on, boy, let's go. Good boy, good boy."

Perro, aroused, bounded out of his dark corner and ran around in circles, barking and jumping up on Pato.

"Down! Down!" shouted the latter, defending himself. "There, that's a good fellow. We'll be ready in a moment."

Behind the bar, Gomez was removing his apron.

"Let's see now," he said, observing himself. "I have put on my sombrero. There is

18

my serape waiting. Here is the gun in my hand ready to be belted on . . . have I forgotten something? Oh, yes, to blow out the lamp." He puffed at the lamp, plunging the Golondrina into still more Stygian shadow. "Now, anything else? Ah, yes, Guillermo. Forgive me, small friend," he said, waving into the general darkness. "Where are you? Come on. No hiding. We are in a hurry."

The fly buzzed in out of the winy gloom, settled in its accustomed place upon the Gomez nose, and commenced to brush its hind legs contentedly. "You have your Perro," — the proprietor remarked — "I have my Guillermo. Let us proceed."

Regretfully Pato shook his head.

"No, *jefe*," he said. "Up in the cold climate of the plateau, Guillermo will not survive. One cold night and . . . poof!"

Gomez closed his eyes, focusing them upon the end of his nose and upon Guillermo.

"Pato is right," he told the fly. "You will have to stay here. Eat the good cheese and get a lot of rest. We won't be away forever."

The fly glared at him with its thousand eyes. It buzzed in a peremptory high tone, then flew over to the cheese.

"I don't know," worried Gomez. "Guillermo is not pleased."

"Look," said Pato hurriedly, "permit me to talk with him. We will enjoy a less emotional relationship. He has his place in society. We are all brothers. I know that I can persuade him, make him see the wrongness and futility of his anger."

"Oh, thank you, Pato. You always understand these things."

"But of course, *jefe.* Take Perro and wait outside."

Gomez whistled to the hulking Perro and departed. Pato turned to the fly.

"Guillermo," he said, "listen. In the nature of things a man must do many acts that may not appear charitable to those who receive the benison. Such a better thing than you are able to comprehend now comes to you."

Pato picked up the piece of bar cheddar upon which Guillermo perched attentively. He stubbed the cheese against the adobe wall, embedding the fly in the rubbery curd. He then went outside and tossed the cheese to Perro, saying: "Catch!"

Perro opened his large mouth and snapped up the tidbit.

"Good boy." Pato nodded.

"You were able to convince Guillermo?" asked Gomez anxiously.

"Absolutely."

"That is nice. He truly wished to go with us. I could see it in all of his eyes."

"Look at it this way, *compadre,*" suggested Pato philosophically. "In a sense you are not leaving him behind. Believe it." He straightened, turning for the river. "Trust in Pato. Forget the Golondrina. Forward, march . . . we are off to the interior."

Gomez and Perro fell in behind him. Gomez was no longer worried. Perro ran in and out of the bottomland brush, flushing cactus sparrows and barking happily. The sky was cerulean blue. The river sparkled in the sunlight. The dust was soft and warm to the bare foot. Everything smelled of summer and success. It was a fine day to begin being bandits.

They followed the river path. Pato, an educated person, was aware that water flowed downhill. He reasoned from this that they had but to follow upward the gentle current of the Río Zorillo to reach the highlands. Being persons of no education, Gomez and Perro found themselves fortunate to be in such learned company. But not even Perro was invulnerable. They had not gone far when he stopped in his tracks.

"*¡Por Dios!*" he cried, striking himself in the forehead. "Do you know what I have forgotten? The horses!"

21

"What horses?" Gomez blinked.

"What horses!" stormed Pato. "Did Pancho Villa *walk* to fame and fortune? Did you ever see a statue of Zapata dismounted? We must have horses!"

"*Sí*, but how can we buy them? We have no *dinero*."

"*Buy* our horses? God's name, Gomez! Since when did bandits buy anything? *¡Por Dios!* We steal them."

"Steal?" Porfirio Gomez grew pale. "You must be crazy, *hombre*. I never stole anything in my life."

Pato flinched visibly. "What do you think it is that bandits do, *amigo?*" he asked. "Borrow?"

"Bandits rob. Anyone knows that."

"Yes, of course. I thought only to be sure you had the distinction clearly in your mind, *jefe*."

"I do. Now how about the horses, Pato?"

"We will rob them."

"Good. Where?"

"Up the river."

"Up the river is only old Esteban Miraflor. He has no horses, only burros."

"We shall see," said Pato. "If he cannot produce mounts, we may need to kill him. Have the gun ready. But right at this time let us go into the river and get cool. Careful

22

with the gun. Don't get it wet. Don't get the bullet wet, either. We don't want it to misfire when we must shoot somebody."

"Yes," said Gomez. "With but a single bullet, one cannot be too careful. I will place it here upon my *pantalones.*"

"Perhaps I had better take the gun. You keep the bullet."

"No, no!" Gomez was not to be so easily taken. "I am the *pistolero!*" He backed away, sheltering the weapon.

Big Perro raised a hand the size of a Yucatán ham. "A true thing, *compañeros,*" he said. "Very true."

"All right. Who cares, anyway? Ready for the water, *amigos?*" Pato, the realist, did not strain at gnats. "Here we go."

"Wait!" It was now Porfirio Gomez who held up the restraining hand. "I just thought of something. This bullet won't fire, anyway. I tried it last summer. It just went clunk. Now what are we going to do if we have to shoot old Miraflor?"

Pato waved the point airily aside. *"Jefe,"* he said, "you are the leader. You don't ask questions. You give orders. Come on, now. Everybody in the water. *¡Hai!*"

Gomez still hesitated, frowning. But Perro gave a happy bark, dropped to all fours, and dashed into the shallows of the stream. Pato, waddling like a duck for which he was named, followed the huge simpleton into the water. Gomez lost his frown. He let the *pantalones* fall the rest of the way. The rusted gun and the verdigrised bullet would wait. So would old man Miraflor and his burros and the whole business of being bandits. Pato was right. The important thing just then was that cool, green river.

"Look out, *amigos!*" he shouted. "Here comes the Tiger of Tehuantltux!"

II

Crouched in the thicket that barricaded the river-bottom *rancho* of Esteban Miraflor, the three desperadoes took pause. Esteban's place was expansive, perhaps as much as an entire acre of cleared ground in its full sweep. Opulence was everywhere. There stood a splendid woodpile containing enough cut wood for at least two meals ahead. Four pigs could be counted, and eleven chickens, eight of which seemed well. There was also a turkey hen and two lame geese, and a milk-goat with a mattered udder. But it was not this wealth of producing livestock that drew the professional eye of the hidden outlaws.

"Aha!" breathed Pato. "What did I tell you? Look at those two beauties over there in the corral! With such fleet steeds beneath us we can laugh at any *rurales* or *federalistas* in the land. Nothing in all of Mexico can match us, not even the swiftest wind.

Which do you choose, *jefe?*"

Gomez scowled. "Of those twins of despair?" he said. "What difference?"

"*Shhh!* Careful. Quiet. They might hear you. Such high-born creatures are all spirit. They have the nerves of lions, the natures of fine beautiful women. Chargers like those must be treated as royalty. Come, my leader. Which will you have of them? The black Spanish Majorca jack or the brown, clean-limbed Sonora jennet?"

"Pato," said Gomez, "you are afflicted. Those are the two burros of old man Miraflor. He calls the one Chapultepec and the other Bustamante."

There was despair in the look that Pato flung him. But there was in the look compassion as well. And some awe.

"The mark of the true *hidalgo,*" he murmured. "He sees the blood and breeding, yet to make his lesser-born companions not to feel ill at ease, he professes to be blind."

"Nevertheless" — Gomez nodded pleasantly — "I still know those two jackasses. Hello, there, Bustamante. Greetings, Chapultepec. It is I, your old friend, Gomez the bandit."

With the salutation, he stepped out of the brush before Pato could seize him. It was too late in any event. The sound of his voice

26

had carried to the adobe hovel from which old Miraflor surveyed his hectares of empire on the banks of the Río Zorillo, rousing the ancient landowner.

"Here! Here!" yelled the old man, tottering out the door. "What is this? Company? Someone comes to visit Esteban Miraflor and goes unwelcomed to his house?"

He stopped short of a curled-up and soundly sleeping mongrel that lay across the door path.

"Get up, you misbegotten rascal!" he screeched at the dog, kicking the beast repeatedly in the ribs and rump. "Strangers and thieves could rob and kill me and you never open an eye. *¡Arriba, arriba!* Do something!"

The bewildered dog, thus set upon, leaped to his feet and rushed about, looking for the enemy or for anything. He saw Gomez just as Pato snatched him back into the thicket. With a brave heart he charged the covert.

"Now you see what you have done, you fat fool!" cried Pato. "Here comes the dog. We are discovered."

"Well," said Gomez, not alarmed, "I cannot imagine what the old man means by setting his dog on us, but if he is going to do that, then we must set our dog loose, also. Go and get them, Perro. I command you."

Perro needed little urging. With a mighty growl he charged out of the thicket. Esteban's cur gave a heart-rending squall of pure fear, turned tail, and raced back toward its peering master. When the latter's rheumy vision made out the sight of huge Perro, running at him upon all fours, the old man fell into a foot race with his dog for the sanctuary of the single acacia tree planted in the ranch yard. Master and brute scrambled up the thorny stem as one and ended huddled together in the higher branches. Perro, leaping and baying at the bole of the acacia, was beneath them.

Seeing the quarry treed, Pato and Gomez quit the thicket and came lumbering up to the scrawny acacia.

"Who is that down there?" called the old man. "And what is that monster you have set upon me and my brave dog? Is it human? Speak up, speak up, or I shall loose my fierce dog upon you again."

"Don't do that, Esteban." Gomez waved. "Save the trouble. It is only I, Porfirio Gomez, the Tiger of Tehuantltux. I and my faithful *teniente,* Pato. This is our friend Perro who leaps at the bole of your nice tree."

"You?" shouted the ancient one, enraged. "Fat Gomez from the Golondrina? What is the meaning of this outrage? What do you want of Miraflor? Be quick with it before I turn loose this vicious dog of mine. He really wants to go at you now, believe it."

"We won't take advantage of your good nature, Esteban," assured Gomez. "We only came to kill you and rob you of your two burros. Come on down. It's very hot, and we have walked a long way up the river."

"Oh, all right," agreed the old man. "But first call off that demented creature at the base of my tree. You better tie him up some place, too. My man-killing dog may want to go after him. But, of course, I will do my best to restrain him. Here I come."

"Many thanks, *viejo,*" said Gomez. "Give me a moment."

He went up to Perro and told him he could stop barking and jumping at the tree. The matter was settled. But Perro was warmed to his work. He turned on Gomez and showed his teeth. The proprietor of the Golondrina backed away, calling upon Pato for protection. The latter looked about. His eye fell upon Esteban's old rat-catcher dozing on the nearby window sill. Picking up the mangy beast, he stroked her a moment, then dropped her upon the ground immediately in front of the growling Perro. The cat swelled up enormously, spit into the eye of the boy giant who was down on all fours, then ran for the goat shed. Perro churned the earth in the eagerness of his pursuit. But no sooner had he raced into the shed than he was back out of it. Now he was yowling in pain, the old cat hooked securely to his nose. There was one visible refuge for Perro, the watering trough beside the burro corral. Into this the big lad dived. Old pussycat, not caring to drown, released her claws and swam for the trough's edge. All the way back to her sunny window sill she shook each wet paw as she picked it up and before she set it down again. She was dozing once more before Perro slinked out of the trough to hide, whimpering, beneath its cover.

"Now," announced Esteban Miraflor, sliding out of the acacia tree, "let us go into my humble *casa* and see what this bandit business is all about. I have a little *aguardiente* saved for just such an important occasion. *Hmmmm,* bandits, you say? Now there's a profession that I have often thought might bring a tidy profit. Yes, yes."

"*¿Aguardiente?*" Pato squinted. "You are sure you said *aguardiente,* host?"

"That's what I said." The old man nodded. "Come on."

They started for the door of the adobe.

"Well, all right," accepted Pato. "We won't need to get to the robbing or the killing in such a hurry. Isn't that what you say, *jefe?*" he inquired of Gomez, who was tagging along absently. "Pleasure before business, eh, my leader?"

Gomez bobbed his bullet head. "Yes, sure," he said, "of course. You heard me. You have your orders, *teniente.*"

"*¿Aguardiente?*" repeated Pato, ignoring him to cling to old Miraflor. "The real *aguardiente?* In a hovel like this? Hard to believe, *viejo.* You must mean *pulque* or perhaps *mescal,* happily."

"*Aguardiente,*" insisted the old man. "A gift from my nephew who is a priest in Ciudad Obregón."

"A lie," said Pato. "But we will call it whatever you wish. God's name," he said, halting just inside the hut, "it is dark as a bat's cave in here. How do you see?"

"When the vision fades with years," replied Miraflor, "light is the enemy of good seeing. One moment, *hombres,* and you will see well enough."

From a place behind the door and, as his two guests stood in the middle of the dirt floor blinking like barn owls to adjust their

31

eyes to the hut's pit-like darkness, the old man plucked a stout cudgel and struck first Pato, and then Gomez expertly and squarely across the backs of their sombreros.

The bandit pair slumped to the floor, senseless.

"Now let me see," said Esteban Miraflor. "Where did I put that jug of *aguardiente?*"

III

The first matter was to dispose of witnesses. The single one of importance was the bumbling giant boy known as Perro. Esteban glanced outside. Perro was still crouched beneath the watering trough. The old man picked up a stick of kindling and stepped outside. Whistling, he attracted Perro's attention. Seeing the stick, Perro came out from under the trough, his troubles with Madame Gata forgotten on the moment. He bounded toward Esteban and made ready to retrieve the stick.

"Aha," said the old fellow soberly. "A fine dog."

He drew back his arm and threw the stick carefully. It sailed in a high arc, Perro setting off barking in vigorous pursuit. The stick made a graceful parabolic curve and slanted downward to fall with a splash into the deep ranch yard well of Esteban Miraflor. Never pausing, the brave Perro leaped after it. The splash he made was larger and more magnificent in every way, but accompanied by a delayed and howling protest that, to a heart less hard than that of the *hacendado* of the Río Zorillo, would have brought immediate humane second thoughts.

"Be patient," advised Esteban Miraflor. "I shall return after a while."

Going inside the house, he carried out the two unconscious bandits and placed them like sacks of shelled corn across the backs of the burros, Bustamante and Chapultepec. Across his own back he slung the jug of *aguardiente.* With a cheery whistle to his ragged mongrel, he was off down the river path, driving the two burros before him.

In due time he came to the old Tehuantltux crossing and the site of the Golondrina. He drove the burros inside the *cantina.* There, he took the still slumbering bodies of Gomez and Pato and propped them up at the dark corner table where Perro customarily dwelled. With care and consummate stinginess, he poured a half cup of *aguardiente* upon the head of each sleeper. Into the tilted-back mouth of the unconscious revelers he poured a very small bit of the fiery liquor, just enough to give them the taste, as he thought of it, as well as the

34

rank odor of the stuff provided by the amount poured over the pates of the two bandits.

Next he put a stub of candle on the corner table and lit it. He lit also the lamp on the bar. Returning to the table, he held the jug of *aguardiente* up to the light, hefting it. Finding it nearly empty, he drained it of its contents, smacked his lips, and laid the emptied jug upon the table between the slack-mouthed celebrants.

Realizing, from some mutterings and stirrings of his would-be assassins, that they were in some danger of regaining their senses, the old man rolled the four barrels of wine which were the Golondrina's entire commercial supply from behind Gomez's bar and fastened them, slung two and two, on the sturdy backs of Chapultepec and Bustamante. Whistling to his dog, he drove the burros out of the *cantina* and back up the riverbank. Within the hour, he was once more returned to his *rancho*.

Storing his plunder in the adobe hut, he windlassed the still-yelping Perro up out of the well and advised him that it was growing dark. "If you wish to reach your home before the moon rises," he said, "you had best be about the journey."

Perro uttered a bark of gratitude and

broke into a lope on all fours down the river path. When, quite soon, he came up to the open doorway of the Golondrina, still wet from the water of old Miraflor's well, he heard the first arousing profanities of his two friends. Rushing inside at once, he jumped up on them, licking their faces and whining eagerly and completing in this manner the awakening of the would-be out-laws.

When Gomez and Pato had cleared their eyes and their brains from the cobwebs of the cudgel blows of Esteban Miraflor's trick upon them, they still could not recall their true plight.

All they knew was that they must have had one memorable celebration upon someone's *aguardiente.* Who might deny it? There before them on the table was the emptied evidence of their great good time — that and the magnificent headaches they were now having. As for the Golondrina, nothing in it appeared to have changed. It was only when, some moments later, Gomez went behind the bar that he discovered the theft of the four barrels of wine. Outraged, he and Pato ran out into the dusty track that passed in front of the Golondrina. Dashing wildly along the sometime road toward the river and toward where the small city of Tehuantltux stood upon the far side of the stream, thcy raised their indignant voices in citizen protest.

"Thief, thief! Help, help!" they cried. "Bandits, bandits! We have been robbed."

Following thcm out of the dirt-floored *cantina,* faithful Perro watched after them, cupping his ear and cocking his shaggy head to hear what it was his good friends shouted with such conviction. When he had made out the sense of the words, the huge boy panted and barked and jumped around delightedly in the dust of the roadway to show his loyal agreement.

"A true thing, *compañeros!*" he shouted in his high voice. "Very true."

Blind Cañon

I

His name was Murrah Starr. He was a friendless, dark-skinned, blue-eyed man who seldom smiled and never laughed. When he talked, his words were slow with a guttural slur at once vaguely familiar yet disturbingly foreign. The men from the creeks and in the camps along the Norton Sound were made uneasy by it and resented it and did not like Murrah Starr because of it.

It was not that alien tongues were strange to them. In the clots of shantied and tented humanity clogging the main artery of the Snake River back from the beach in that second of Nome's blustery autumns, the harsh accents of foreign speech were more common by two-to-one than the good nasal sounds of American English. From the thin, far echo of the discovery cry the bleak desolation of Norton Sound's north strand had been inundated with a flood of offshore and inland immigrants. There were heavy-voiced Russians from the sealing posts of the Pribilof Islands, Swedes, Danes, and Norwegians from the Arctic-prowling Old World whalers, swart Genoese, blond Latvians, slant-eyed Malay lascars, and nut-brown Pacific Islanders from the ship-jumping deck crews of the tall-masted traders. Canadian Englishmen were up from British Columbia, French Canucks from Quebec by way of the Horn and San Francisco, burly Scots and broguing Irish from the Oregon timber slashes. Poles, Prussians, Greeks, Bulgars came fluxing up from the States through the funneling cesspool of Seattle's overflowing waterfront. They were all there, all grudgingly tolerated that fall of 1899. Add to them the hundreds of returning inlanders, lapping back down the Yukon from the thinning gravels of the Klondike, and the "beach at Babylon" was complete. Indeed, not by a score of distant sources and unfamiliar tongues was the sea-borne immigrant Cheechako or Yukon-descending sourdough a stranger to Nome's wild melting pot.

The simple trouble was that Murrah Starr was no offshore immigrant, or inland sourdough. He came not from any sailing ship's deserting crew, or from any foundering

42

tramp steamer's Stateside passenger list. He had been there when it began, or before it began. No one really knew. He had simply materialized out of the vast interior beyond White Horse, beyond Dawson, beyond Skagway, accompanied only by the sullen shadow of Smoke, his high-withered wolf dog. He had staked his claim and located it among the first ten recorded by the original Miners Association, long months before the discovery.

They said he was a Chinik or a Selawik Indian half-breed, or a white-fathered Tubucktulik Eskimo, or a renegade half-blood Canuck. If they were right, or partly right, it was only the covetous hazard of a resentful guess. For Murrah Starr never told them what he was or where he had come from. The only thing they knew about him was the thing no man can keep a secret from a bonanza camp's merciless twenty-four hour espionage of the trading companies' weighing scales.

His Blind Cañon Mine, hidden somewhere inland of fabulous Anvil Creek, was recorded cryptically as "east drainage upper Pushtash north and south to the stakes." And that was all. Not another comma of written locating description, or a solitary added spoken word. No one had ever heard of Pushtash Creek; no one had ever succeeded in following him there. But he weighed his gold in nuggets as big and rough-edged as smelter cinders, and his finest dust was grainier than beach-run sand. The answer was simple. Murrah Starr's Pushtash pocket had to be the richest single strike in American Alaska.

At the town's edge, Starr loosened his pack harness, shoved his old .45-90 Springfield under the worn webbing. He spoke to the wolf dog, a grunting command that had no meaning in English, and the brute slunk to heel, staying there. They went along Front Street's piling-supported tents and shanties, disdaining the newly raised boardwalk, slogging through the rutted mud. Beyond them, the rasping aorta of Nome's whiskey-quickened heart flared to pump its overflow onto the open, treeless beach.

Starr could dimly see, through the clouded gray of the Northern midnight, the shadows of the big ships anchored in the ocean roadstead beyond the shelving drop-off of the Snake's estuary. In the river anchorage itself, along the rickety tide-flung lightering piers, lay the flotsam of smaller boats, steam tugs, barges, dinghies, catboats, and Indian *umiaks* born to suckle the cargo from the parent ships and spew it nauseously on the beach. Out past them, even in the middle of the night, a score of their parasitic sisters rowed and sputtered through the surf, scuttling around the clock to ferry in the endless stream of gold seekers and the piled mountains of supplies that would keep them half alive through the coming time of the long night and the isolating crush of the soon-to-form polar ice pack.

Starr liked what he saw. His sometime smile flicked once across his wide lips and was gone. It was late in September. Already the first storm was gusting in, black and rain-wet from the Bering Strait, whipping up the salt chop across Norton Sound. Those ships out there were the last ones. They brought the last of the winter's supplies, the last of the sea-borne invaders. After them would come the pack ice, bridging inward from the offshore floes. Nothing more of the outside world would come to Nome until the pack buckled and broke to the pale spring sun. But before it did, there would be those great, quiet, friendly months in which God's calm solitude would return to the frozen diggings and in which certain death by cold and privation would stalk among the crowd-foul hundreds on Nome's naked beach.

That was good, Starr thought. Very good.

There were already far too many there, upwards of 3,000 at the end of that second summer. The real rush would come next year with the open water of 1900's spring. Then would be seen a tidal wave from the States that would make the present brawling backwash from Seattle and the played-out Yukon bars seem like a summer shower. Those present few thousands were largely accidents of time and place, hardy adventurers who had been within striking distance in the pursuit of their normal hard professions when the magic word went out. True, a goodly part of them were Cheechakos even then, but the percentage of the latter would be overwhelming in the third summer's influx unless something happened meantime to dull their appetites for easy millions. That something could be the coming winter, provided it was severe enough. Hunching his narrow shoulders to the increasing bite of the Bering Strait wind, Murrah Starr thought the approaching storm gave good and early promise of bringing just such a winter.

His dark smile flicked again. This time, however, his enjoyment of it was interrupted. Glancing ahead, his restless eyes tightened suddenly. He spoke sharply to the wolf dog in that strange tongue, not altering his long stride. The latter raised his snake-flat head, swung it in the direction of his master's gaze. He whined once, and trembled, then was quiet.

Up the street, quartering across it from their skulking among the fish-heads and frozen garbage dumped between Boozer Brown's just-finished saloon and the still unpainted Northern Lights Hotel, drove a ranging pack of settlement mongrels. There were six or eight of them, hard-culled fugitives from Nome's insatiable hunger for useable pack and sled animals. They were coming, guard hairs on end, squealing their eagerness for the stranger.

When their leader, a handsome Kugruk River Husky without the shame of fear or memory of defeat in him, was thirty feet away, Starr stopped. Smoke looked up at him, whined again. Starr nodded, stepped aside. Too late, the Kugruk got the wolf smell of the alien. He tried to swerve, but Smoke struck him shoulder-on, knocking him in under the stilt-raised boardwalk. He was after him like a great gray ferret. There was no sound from Smoke and only one strangled squall from his would-be attacker. The stricken Husky wobbled back out onto the street, went down in the mud, kicking limply.

The following pack was on top of Smoke then, whimpering and crying in their eagerness to kill him. They came off of him as fast, rear legs scrabbling to escape, fearful yells noising their belated discovery of the smell that had come too late to their leader. The Kugruk was still bubbling bloody froth from his torn throat when the last of his scavenger pack had fled back into the alley and the first of the passing boardwalk stragglers were gathering behind the motionless figure of Murrah Starr.

"McClennon ain't going to like this," announced someone in the crowd. "He set a heap of store by that dog."

"He did and that's a fact," answered someone else. "I'd hate to be in your moccasins, stranger."

Newcomers, Cheechakos, thought Starr, and did not bother to answer them. He had not been in town more than three times all summer, would not be in it any longer than it took him to make up his winter pack and get back out. He had no time and little temper for the opinions of tinhorns. But the crowd was not composed entirely of tenderfeet.

"Ain't that the god-damn' Injun from up the crick?" he heard one bearded old-timer ask his companion.

48

"Yeah, him and his sneaking pet wolf," the other miner sneered. "I'd give twenty dollars an ounce to be there when McClennon hears about this."

Now Starr came around, facing them, his dark face blank. "Save your money," he told them. He went into the street, picked up the dead dog by the tail, stared up at them again. "Follow along, you'll get a free show."

He started off, Smoke at heel, the Husky's bloody head and forelegs dragging in the mud behind him. The men came after him, hesitantly at first, then with a crowding shove as he went in the door of McClennon's mercantile.

Angus McClennon, a black-browed, bad-tempered, second generation Scot, was at the counter scales, weighing out a poke for a creek miner. When he saw Starr and the dead dog, he put the half-emptied buckskin pouch on the scales, moved out around the counter, and set himself on legs as thick and squat as blue spruce stumps.

"Put him down, mon," he murmured pleasantly. The smooth, slight burr of his Highland sire that lingered in his deep voice did not confuse Starr. There was Celtic murder burning in the pitchblende darkness of his small eyes. Starr put the dog down.

"He came at us." He nodded, first indicating the dead Husky, then his own dog.

McClennon looked at the wolf dog where he sat, tongue lolling, slant eyes half closed with boredom, on guard at the door. Behind him, he noticed how the onlookers were backed into a nervous straggle along the wall, careful to give the gaunt brute all the room his silent watchfulness seemed to suggest as the reasonable minimum.

"I gave a Golovin Bay Eskimo two hundred dollars in trade goods for that dog two weeks ago. Aye, and he was a natural leader, if ever ye saw one." He nodded to Starr, taking off his plaid blanket coat as he talked. "How do ye want to pay for him, Starr?"

"I'm sorry," said the latter. "I didn't know he was your dog. I haven't been in town since you got him. He came at us." He shrugged. "I told Smoke to take him."

McClennon folded his coat, laid it carefully on the counter. "I asked ye a civil question, mon. How do ye want to pay for the dog? Yer own gray brute, or yer dirty teeth knocked down yer half-breed throat?"

"I don't want to pay for him any way," said the other, low-voiced. "I got a dog."

The huge Scot shook his head slowly. "Ah, no, now, laddie. Ye've no dog there." His thick arm went over the counter, came up with a short-barreled Winchester carbine. He levered the action. "Step aside, now, if ye will. Ye're covering him."

Only Starr's thin lips moved. "I'll kill you if you try it."

Again the other's massive head wagged slowly. "It's yer choice. Ye or yer slant-eyed wolf. How'll ye have it?"

Starr looked at him, turned his hunted eyes on the circle of waiting miners, brought them back to the hulking trader. "You're a fool, McClennon," he said, and unslung his pack and his Springfield.

He dropped them to the floor, armed out of his fox-fur parka, let it fall on top of them, slid the whole pile aside with his foot and without looking down. He shook his shoulders to get the set of the trail out of them, flexed his copper-skinned hands, slid forward.

Behind him, as he did, Smoke came up off his haunches, housing his wet tongue with a trapping *click* of his blunt jaws. Mc-Clennon centered him with the Winchester. "Put the wolf outside," he told Starr softly. "I'll not fight any mon with such a beast behind him."

Starr's dark face colored. "I'm sorry," he muttered awkwardly. "I forgot him. Smoke. . . ."

The wolf dog shot his stumpy ears forward, froze with one reaching forefoot in mid-air.

"Ya howo," ordered the half-breed in his strange tongue. Smoke stared unblinkingly at Starr, growling deeply in his throat. *"Ya howo!"* repeated Starr harshly.

To the tensely watching miners it seemed as though the scarred brute actually nodded in receipt of the guttural command. A chill went through them. They faded back out of the way as the swarthy owner of the Blind Cañon Mine gestured warningly. "Kick open the door and stand clear of him."

One of the men reached gingerly to unhook the spring latch, nudged the door open with his boot. Smoke slid through the narrow opening and was gone. The catch snapped behind him.

"We'll have it your way," said Murrah Starr. From the way he said it, going forward bent-kneed and crouching toward McClennon, the second chill in as many sharpened breaths ran through the silent watchers.

II

At first they circled as old dogs and wise men will. While they did, the men along the wall pulled in, instinctively surrounding them in response to that law of the pack that was already old when the first slope-skulled cave dweller picked up a rock and went for the second. McClennon had the inside of the circle and the advantage. He held the position, forcing Starr to go wide around him. The latter seemed strangely content with this pattern, made no opening move to alter it.

He glided around the huge Scot once, twice, began a third cautious circuit. The low sound that at once ran the backing crowd was an animal growl. The damned half-breed was afraid! He was stalling, not knowing what to do, lacking the insides either to go for McClennon, or to face them and admit he did not have the belly to fight a white man from the front.

Again the angry growl muttered through them. They were all alike, these sneaking half-bloods. Just enough white in them to give them the idea they were as good as anybody. Too much of the other color to give them the simple guts to go about proving it. The third growl ran ugly and deep.

Starr heard it and understood it. He knew what the miners were thinking and, glancing uneasily at his slowly turning opponent, knew they had full reason for the thought. Black Angus McClennon was as big as a Kodiak Island bear. He had the temper of a Kotzebue malamute, the strength of a 260-pound wolverine. He was a famous and fearful hand fighter, had killed one man and crippled a dozen in just such bare-knuckle traps as that in which he had now had Starr caught. There was no escape except to follow Smoke through that locked door. A man knew that, and knew, as well, that, when he did follow the wolf dog out, he would not remember it. For some unknown reason McClennon meant to kill him.

It was his instinctive sensing of this fact, not his fear of it, that slowed the half-breed's step. Why, suddenly, after all these watchful, waiting months of trying to trail him to his hidden mine, would the murderous owner of the mercantile want to kill him? Something had happened since his last trip in to change McClennon's scheming mind and patient, crafty plan. It was certainly not the dead Husky or his normal white man's hatred of half-breeds. Could it be then that he had — no, that was impossible! No settlement miner turned boomtown merchant, no white man of any trade, could trail Murrah Starr. He shook off the ugly possibility of the big Scot's having discovered the location of his mine. He even forced aside the warning thought that the latter intended to beat him to death, legally, in front of friendly witnesses. He had been wrong, too fearful, too suspicious. He could go on in now and get it over with. Halfway around the third circle, he whirled and slashed in at the ponderous, heavy-shouldered trader.

But McClennon's bulk was deceptive. He had the reflexes of a hunting cat, and he was ready. He grunted, grinned, set himself, drove a fist the size and hardness of an oak burl straight into the dark face. Yet the face was not there when the fist was. The raking blow tore across Starr's drooping shoulder, throwing the big Scot momentarily off balance. Starr's shoulder came in below his belt, lifted twistingly up and back. McClennon's thick body went up in the air, crashed heavily to the floor. He was on his feet instantly, unhurt and only made uglier by the surprise and embarrassment of the fall.

So the half-breed was a wrestler. Good. Aye, that made it simpler. The man who could only grapple and gouge and use his hands for taking body holds had small chance against the one who understood how to smash with his. He ground his knotted fist in his palm, started the second grin, stepped into Starr.

This time his blow was a feinted repeat of the first one. Starr was deceived by it. As he repeated his own shoulder-twisting maneuver, the following, left fist hooked into his body and drove up under his heart. He gasped, straightened, his face the color of a rotten salmon's belly. The feinting fist recovered, exploded into his open mouth. There was the better part of 300 pounds of Celtic bone and muscle behind it. Starr's slender form buckled and snapped like a curling dog whip. He fell backward, caromed off the counter behind him, stumbled blindly over a bale of fox furs, sprawled headlong. He was still conscious, but helpless, when the Scot's sealskin boot drove into his ribs.

The greenstick *crunch* of the fracturing bones tortured through him. The shock and pure intense pain of it emptied his adrenals. The discharge of the glands burst through his back and shoulders and the pit of his gut. Suddenly there was no more pain. The paralysis was gone. He saw the second boot coming, writhed toward it, seized it in mid-air. He came up with it, wrenching savagely.

McClennon roared with the hurt of it, even as he was falling. The following crash of his shaggy head against a convenient barrel of pick handles did nothing to improve his fury, or the odds in his favor of the easy victory he had anticipated. He made no attempt to control the former, but, as he regained his feet, his trained brawler's mind reacted to increase the latter. The third grin was spreading as his big hand reached behind him to close about one of the carved hickory shafts in the barrel.

Hefting it, sizing it, reveling in the good feel of it in his hand, already hearing the skull crush of its coming impact with the half-breed's unprotected head, he moved lumberingly forward. Starr, waiting for him, had a bad decision to make.

The pick handle changed everything. He had only one counter weapon within reach. To use it meant certain defeat even if, in that use, he managed to down his opponent for keeps. Not to use it meant a broken head and a rush and roar of darkness that would never end. For there could be no remaining doubt now. McClennon did mean to kill him.

He reacted to the oldest urge a man knows. The first law was to live. The gleam of his hidden sheath knife flashed from its undershirt neck thong, drove in under the down-sweeping arc of McClennon's blow. He could have killed the big man, then, as easily as finishing off a crippled caribou. Deliberately he did not, but instead aimed the strike wide and cut him, deep and clean, through the side-fat below the ribs. Mc-Clennon screamed, spun half around, dropped the pick handle, clutched his spurting side. The miners closed on Starr before he could recover from the thrust.

He remembered the swarm of their sweated bodies, the face-close heat of their cursing breath. Then, the tearing of the knife from his relaxing hand, the uncounted blows of their knees and fists, the last painless feeling of their kicking him to the floor and his jerking struggle to raise up once more at the fading sight of McClennon, coming at him again with the pick handle. That was all.

After that he was floating free and easy somewhere far out under the Arctic stars. It was a place he had never seen before and he saw no landmarks that were familiar to him. Just the quiet and the dark and the motionless peace of the void around him. That and the sense of uncrowded time that came with it, and the suspended, no longer important or useful thought of the crime that had brought him to this restful nothingness.

In a fair fight a white man could use any weapon he could close his hairy fist upon. A shattered chair, a broken bottle, a crowbar, an axe, a pick handle, all were good, clean, and sportful advantages under frontier settlement rules. But by those same rules, the one weapon you were denied was precisely the one you had been raised and trained with and best understood if you were a "lousy blue-eyed half-breed". It was the natural defense weapon of the dark-skinned, as instinctive to them as the balled fist to the Caucasian. Maybe that was why the latter had made the law the way it was. Maybe not. To argue the difference was pointless. The law was there; you knew about it; you had broken it; it had killed you.

III

But Murrah Starr was not dead. There was still life in him when they dragged him out of the mercantile and dumped him over the boardwalk into the mud-ditched gutter. Not much, it was true. Not nearly enough for any of the miners to detect. Only enough for the snarling wolf dog to sense and to crouch by and stand guard over.

The half-breed's beaten body attracted only the attention necessary for the pedestrian traffic to step over it and for the mounted traveler to swing his horse around it to avoid trampling it. The forms of drunken or half-dead men lying along the boardwalks of Front Street were no novelty to a town where the real dead ones were commonplace. The only law between the Yukon and Fish River was U.S. Marshal Harry LaMont, and he was somewhere over toward Golovin Bay, running out a Stateside murder warrant. LaMont had two deputies in Nome, but the only law they looked after was the one of free whiskcy supply and demand at the Forty Mile or Gus Siefert's bar. Under ordinary circumstances a man could lie in Front Street all that second winter through and not be touched by friend or foe until the spring thaw — and only then because with warm weather the smell got high enough to be bad for business.

However, Erin Eileen O'Farrell was scarcely an ordinary circumstance. To have called her one would have been to name the northern lights, the Arctic stars, or the midnight sun run-of-the-mill. At least, so thought Murrah Starr when he opened his puffed eyes and saw her oval face burning through the thinning haze above him.

Starr had never had the nerve for good women, or the time for bad ones. He was twenty-three years old and had yet to touch his first one of either kind. Not that the hunger was not in him like it was in any man. It was, fierce and hot and strong. Sometimes, beside the loneliness of the out-trail fires, with the south wind fresh in the spruce tops bringing the smell of a softer spring from far places, it got so bad a man could feel it almost killing him. Yet it was just those times that made Starr know what the difference was between them and him. For white men it was simple; they only wanted a woman. Starr knew he must have a mate.

Above him now, the haze thinned still more, faded, was gone altogether. The girl's face came into clear, breath-catching focus. For a long time Murrah Starr could say nothing.

Erin O'Farrell was not a beautiful woman. She was something far more disturbing than that. Her face was that of a pagan, her body that of a savage. Her hair was as dark as Starr's, her eyes were jarringly blue, her mouth as wide and sensuous. Her cheek bones were as high and angular, her small ears as flat and close to her head. Her skin. . . . It was there that Starr's excitement jolted to a stop. Her skin was white — and pure as the under snow of winter's first fall. That was what struck him in mid thrill, and what was to haunt him mercilessly from that instant on. He knew, in the magic of that first second, that he had found her, realized, with the next bitterly indrawn breath, what a cruel finding it really was.

After all the lonely fires and faraway nights, the winds of southern chance had brought him a white woman! His jaw tightened clenchingly. The movement, slight as it was, shocked his mind from the girl back to himself. He winced with the pain, began remembering a few things. His first thought was for Smoke.

"Where's the dog?" he demanded, struggling to sit up.

At the sound of the words, he heard the answering rumble of the familiar growl. The next moment he felt the inquiring shove of the moist black nose, saw the great, wedge-shaped head withdraw and cock itself with the worried whine. "Good dog," he gritted, "lie down."

The wolf dog dropped to his belly beside the bed and Starr sank back weakly.

"How in God's name did you get him here?" he inquired idly. Then, with gathering concentration: "For that matter, how did you get me here? And why?"

"Dogs like me." The girl smiled in answer to the first question, and her voice made Starr think of the south wind in the spruce tops again.

"They don't like him." He managed to grin stiffly, nodding toward Smoke.

"What do you mean?" she said, puzzled.

"He's not a dog, miss, not bred or born or raised one. I took him out of a trap when he was better than a yearling cub. He's pure wolf, miss."

She looked at Smoke, edged away from him with the doubtful smile. "Well, pure or not, he didn't give me any trouble. But I was given to understand that you might."

Starr scowled suspiciously. "Maybe you understand quite a bit I don't. Maybe you'd better get started catching me up on some of it."

"Maybe I had," she said, and gave it to him untrimmed,

"They've given you a blue ticket, mister."

He took it unblinkingly, but it was bad, very bad. The blue ticket was judge, jury, and automatic verdict of guilty in lawless Nome. When the Miners Association hung it on you, it meant get out and stay out, or else.

"Who told you so?" he asked.

"LaMont's deputies. They helped me get you over here to my place."

"And . . . ?"

"They said you tried to kill the wrong man in the mercantile. They said you'd understand."

He understood all right, a lot more than this girl or any of the rest of them figured he did. But to her he only nodded. "Mc-Clennon?"

"Yes. They said to tell you he called a Miners Association meeting right after the fight and got the membership to vote you a ticket. They said you'd understand they had no choice but to make that ticket stick, and that you wouldn't want to make things any tougher for them than they already were."

Again Starr nodded. That was for sure, as the ice went out of the river on break-up day. Once the Association pinned the blue ticket on a man, he had two choices: get out of town or spend the winter in Nome's jail.

Starr knew that jail. Situated across the river on the Snake's seaward sand spit, west of Eskimo Town, it went unheated from October to April, save for a single oil drum converted to smolder soft coal and snow-wet driftwood scraps. Its inmates were fed like Chinik Indian dogs — a chunk of frozen salmon thrown through the bars every twenty-four hours, with a pot of melted snow water to wash it down. It was no better than a death sentence to be put in that jail after the snow began to fly.

"I understand it," he said at last. "But how about you? Where's your personal stake in all this, lady?"

She flushed at his bluntness, her quick anger flaring back at him. "I wouldn't leave a dog lying in Front Street on a night like this. Or" — she added scathingly, with a slender finger at the attentive Smoke — "a wolf!"

He listened to the lash of the rain against the shack's single window. "It's a bad night, all right. Especially for this early in the fall. It'll likely turn into snow before morning."

"Well, let it," she murmured, a little ashamed of her sharpness. "We'll worry about it then. You've got to rest now." She touched him on the shoulder, pressing him back.

Starr came as close as he ever did to laughing when she said that. He swung his legs to the floor, gasping at the grinding hurt of his torn ribs. "Lady," he grunted, "you haven't been up here very long, have you?"

"Five weeks. Why?" She tilted her chin at him.

He ignored her. "How long have I been resting here?" he asked cynically.

"About an hour. It's two o'clock now. It was a little after one when I saw you trying to crawl up on the boardwalk in front of the mercantile."

He bobbed his lean head. "I've got to get out of here, miss. And fast. Likely they followed you and LaMont's men."

Something in the hunted, desperate look of him got to her. "Go on," she heard herself

66

saying. "If you're in trouble, you can trust me."

As she said it, her black-lashed eyes caught and held his. It was a long, deliberate stare and Starr felt it go into him. But he fought down the wild thought it stirred up in him. For a crazy minute there, a man got the idea that she, too, had smelled the south wind and sat to her share of lonely fires. But that was twisted thinking. She was a white woman. Again he forced the thought away. Still it would not go down. Indeed, it could not, for she was still looking at him, still waiting for him, and those blue-green eyes were talking a language older than both of them.

It was suddenly in him, full and strong, to do as she said — to trust her — all the way and like he had never trusted another human in all his hard life. "All right, miss," he began, his guttural voice thickening its peculiar slurring accent as it quickened. "I've got to trust somebody. My name's Murrah Starr and I am in trouble, big trouble."

"You mean the fight, Mister Starr?"

"That, yes. But past that and before it, too. I've got a mine, miss, the richest one since they rockered the first batch of Klondike gravel back in 'Ninety-Six. Nuggets big and burry as horse chestnuts! Dust coarser than grit in a wild duck's craw!" His eyes blazed and hers took fire from them.

"I've heard of you. They call you the Indian!"

"The god-damn' Indian," corrected Starr, and swept on. "McClennon's after that mine, miss, and now he's got what he's been needing, a proper excuse to take it away from me. At least I heard as much up the creeks. It's partly why I came to town, to check on it."

"On what? What are you talking about?"

"Up in the diggings they're saying McClennon has got the Association to pass a resolution keeping foreigners from owning claims. You hear anything about that?"

"Yes, it's true I guess. But I don't believe they mean it. They haven't done anything yet."

"They've been waiting to hear from the government on it. Now they say the rumor's beat the official ruling back. The government isn't going to back them on it."

"Yes, I've heard that, too."

Starr's blue eyes darkened. His narrow jaw muscled sharply, as he bit the words off. "So has McClennon."

She shook her head, irritated by the bobtailed reference. "If I'm going to help you,

you'll simply have to stop talking like . . ."
— she hesitated awkwardly, finished half
defiantly — "well, like an Indian!"

She had not meant it to hurt him, a man
could sense that and accept it, from her.

"I'll try," he said. "To begin with, Mc-
Clennon is a pure bad one. He's got a dozen
of the best claims up along Anvil Creek. He
didn't file on a one of them originally, and
there hasn't been anybody heard any complaints from them that did. It's pretty hard
to object after you've been dumped under
the river ice with two, three rifle slugs
through the back of your head."

"I don't believe it!" Again her indignation
was honest and he let her finish. "You can't
make me believe Angus McClennon is a
common murderer!"

"You're right, miss, he isn't. He's an
uncommon one. Let me ask you a question.
Do you really think he tried to kill me
tonight, just on account of Smoke downing
his dog?"

"I don't know. I just don't know what to
think," she admitted frankly.

"Well, you listen and I'll tell you," he said
grimly. He stood up, the effort beading his
dark forehead with sweat. "I'm next on Mc-
Clennon's list. He's been after my diggings
from the first, but has never been able to

find them up to now. I've been followed back out every time I came in for supplies, a couple of times by boys who never got back to the mercantile to turn in their traveling expenses."

She looked at him, white-faced. "You killed two men?"

"Let's just say I got a good close look at them when they weren't doing any looking back. They were McClennon's friends."

"And you call *him* a murderer . . . ?" There was not only disbelief and righteous anger in her voice now, but fear as well. That hurt him but still he made no effort to argue the moral distinction. "He knows he's got to hurry now, before official word of the government turn-down on his no foreigners resolution gets back here. Once his American citizens only swindle is officially thrown out, it makes it that much tougher for him to jump my claim and get away with it. You can see that, can't you?"

"No, I can't!" she snapped. "What's that silly resolution got to do with you? Whether it's been refused or not. You're certainly not a foreigner!"

"No," he answered her, hard-eyed, "and I'm not an American citizen, either."

"What do you mean by that?" she demanded, again made impatient by his oblique statements.

He looked at her witheringly. "You ever hear of an Indian that was a citizen, miss?"

"Then you *are* an Indian?"

"They say I am. That makes me one."

"So?"

"So up here things are no different for an Indian than they were in the States thirty years ago. McClennon's bunch figures they can use me to set up a good example of the way their resolution ought to work. And when they say good in connection with an Indian, they've got only one kind of an Indian in mind, a dead one. That's me, miss."

"And what does that mean?" She frowned.

"Only one thing it can mean. They've somehow found the Blind Cañon. They don't need me alive any more, and they're pushing to prove it before bad word gets back from Washington. It's why McClennon tried to kill me, miss."

She still did not believe it. "But how can you know that, Mister Starr? Men fight all the time up here. I see them lying in the street every night. That doesn't mean someone deliberately tried to murder them."

"Doesn't it, miss?" he said softly. "You saw me on that boardwalk tonight. You know McClennon put me there. Did it look to you like he meant for me ever to get up off of it?"

She shuddered, remembering the whimpering, hurt animal sounds which had led her to bend over his broken body. And remembering the look in his eyes when he had first opened them to stare up at her. Her angular face was suddenly soft, her frown was gone and her doubts of him swept under by all her normal woman's compassion for the hurt, the lonely, the hunted thing.

"I'll help you, Starr. I've told you that. What do you want me to do?"

He did not miss the unconscious dropping of the "mister" and again the quick thrill shot his spine. "I've got to have a new rifle, miss." He brought out a heavy buckskin poke, thrust it into her hand. "A Winchester. One of the new ones. They're the Model Ninety-Fours. Get it in Forty-Four caliber if you can."

"Where will I buy it?"

"Bengstrom's. That's the main hardware three doors past the Northern Lights. Pick a clerk who doesn't know you and have him wrap it in regular brown paper, no case or anything."

"All right," she murmured, understanding that he did not dare go himself. "How will I get it to you?"

He limped over to the wolf dog, took a short chain out of the dog pack the gaunt animal carried. He snapped it to his choke-chain collar, fastened him to the leg of the wall bunk. "I'll leave Smoke here," he said. "You load him with all the cartridges you can tote back from Bengstrom's. Get a whole, unbroken case if you can." He paused, setting his jaw at the uncertainty of the rest of it, but having no choice. "You know the Anvil Creek trail?"

"No, but I'll learn it!"

His dark smile flicked at the way she said it, making her feel warm and strange and oddly excited.

"Good. You head up there with the gun. When you get to the main diggings, eight, ten miles out, you ask somebody to set you on the Dry Gulch cut-off. Follow that straight on up."

"Where will I see you?"

"You won't. I'll see you."

In the little stillness that followed, Smoke brought his huge head up from the floor, growling ugly and deep. Starr tensed, following the set of the wolf dog's ears toward the door and the alley outside. *"Tinga!"* he hissed, and the growl shifted into the thin eager wolf whimper that had preceded the death of McClennon's dog. "They're out there," he told the girl, "watch it!" He ducked beneath the window, listened at the door, glided back. "Keep clear of that window and uncover your ears!" he went on, low-voiced. He was smiling again, but somehow there was no mirth in it and it put a shiver through the settlement girl that she could feel clear to her fingertips. "You load Smoke up with the cartridges and turn him loose as soon as you get back from the store. He'll find me, don't worry. Then you set out after him with the gun, soon as the storm lets up tomorrow." He gritted his white teeth, chopping off the smile. "I hate to bring you into this, miss, but Smoke can't pack the rifle . . . no way to lace it on him that it wouldn't hamper him. Too long and off balancing. Apt to spook him bad and get him all tangled and fouled with himself. You got to bring it or I don't get it."

"You'll get it," she promised excitedly. "I'll go buy it first thing in the morning."

Starr shook his head. "They're open all night, miss. You buy it right now, while this rain's got it good and black outside and nobody'll see you toting it back home. You can start downtown as soon as I'm gone. Meanwhile, you can start getting your clothes off."

"My what off?" she gasped, eyes widening at the outrageous suggestion. His sharp scowl cut her off. "You heard me, miss. Your clothes. All of them. They think I'm still in here. You've got to make them think otherwise. Undressing like you were getting ready for bed is the best way I know to accomplish that. See you do it in front of the window curtain, with the lamp behind you, so they can get the idea good and clear." He turned his back on her. "Now, miss."

She gasped again, flushed, felt her throat swell and hammer with the pressure of the thought of standing naked in the same room with this strange, dark savage. But she knew she was going to do what he had asked, and that he knew she was.

Behind him, Starr heard dropping to the floor things that he had seen only in the mail-order catalogues at the mercantile. After a long minute he heard her draw aside the thin curtain and thought she was ready and through and had gotten out of her street clothes and into her nightgown. He was wrong. Her voice caught him in a half turn.

"My gown's on the hook there by you. Over the bed."

He saw the flimsy garment, picked it from its hanger, dropped it to the floor, and kicked it behind him. He heard the light sound of her bare feet moving to get it, and knew she had gone all the way for him in distracting McClennon's watchdogs outside the window, and in convincing them that she was alone in the little cabin. She had, in the last minute of her disrobing, deliberately opened the shabby curtain and allowed them to see her slip into the nightgown, with nothing between her slim body and their hungry eyes but ten-dollars' worth of San Francisco window glass. "I'm beholden," he managed to mutter at last, clumsily, breaking the painful silence.

It was the first time he had heard her laugh, and it was like the rest of her, rich and warm and a little wild. "I'll bet you are!" she said. "And your friends out there, too! Either that or they're blind." She was moving again with the words. The lamp went out. The wick smoke guttered upward, pungent, sooty black. Her voice touched him on the shoulder.

"It's all right, now. . . ."

He came around in the bat-dark, not seeing her but sensing and smelling her there in front of him. Impulsively his lean hands reached out. In finding her shoulders, they brushed the curving side thrust of her hard breasts. She trembled but did not move. His hands dropped to her upper arms, tightened, gripped hard for a hushed moment, fell away.

"All right," he answered, and slid past her toward the door. She followed him, the silence so intense she could her the wincing sound of his broken ribs grating as he bent below the window. Behind them, the wolf dog whimpered again, wrinkling his blunt nose through the darkness to follow Starr's scent, his feathery plume thumping the floorboards eagerly. "Down," whispered Starr, "stay here."

Smoke dropped at the end of his chain, yellow eyes boring the cabin blackness, never leaving the blurred shadow of his master's movements.

At the door, Starr raised the latch, swung the weathered planks six inches inward, peered out into the drive of the rain. After a long moment he cursed softly, eased the door closed again.

"You there, girl?"

"Right here." The powdery voice was at his elbow.

"One more thing. You see you get out and back quick as you can. I don't like the way this wind is shifting out to sea. Front Street will be under four feet of salt tidewater inside the next two hours. Don't let it catch you dragging your feet."

"I won't. Oh, I won't. . . ."

He creaked the door back open, wider this time. "Bolt it after me," he said. Then, very slow and halting, his odd accent thickening: "I'll remember you, miss."

"Starr . . . !"

He stopped, halfway through the opening, lean shoulders squared against the lesser black of the rain darkness. "Yes, miss?"

"My name is Erin O'Farrell. I'm your friend. Remember that!"

He did not turn and she saw his shoulders slacken, as the strength and the squareness went out of them. "You're a white woman," she heard him say. "You can't be my friend." Then, bitterly soft: "You remember that . . . !"

When she called after him, guarded and low and fierce into the sheeting rain, there was only the eerie whistle of the September wind to answer her. Murrah Starr was gone.

IV

Starr slid along the shack's wall, keeping to the higher ground that ridged along the alley's buildings leading to Front Street, his mind casting ahead through the rain gusts that his eyes could not penetrate. If any of McClennon's men had been left to guard the alley, they would be at its Front Street end, knowing that the rain had already closed its other, open end, leading to the tundra behind Nome. The alley was not over twelve feet wide but visibility was less than half that. If they had set a guard up ahead, a man had first to guess where that guard would be. Then he had to do better than that. He had to know that his guess was right.

Thinking of the alley's entrance, Starr guessed that any remaining watchers, being only white men and no doubt at least partially convinced by the girl's act of undressing in front of the window that he was no longer in her cabin, would be taking advantage of what rain shelter they had available. That would be the roofed-over boardwalk in front of the Alaska Commercial Company's warehouse on the opposite, south corner of the alley.

He held up just short of that corner on the north side of the narrow thoroughfare. A long ten seconds of intent listening brought no human sound through the increasing slash of the rain. Damn. That was no good. He had hoped to hear voices, letting him know his guess was correct. He waited another whole minute, still heard nothing. Well, that was that. Now he had to find out the risky way.

He felt along the rickety side of the building he was standing against. Presently he found what he wanted — a loose board. He felt its length and heft, judged the amount of noise it would make breaking loose. Both measurements came out right. Setting himself, he split the timber free of its rusting nails.

"What the hell was that?" The low query came from across the alley, and Starr grinned.

"I dunno. Sounded like a sideboard blowing loose. Want I should take a look?"

"Yeah, you'd best," came a third voice,

and the half-breed slid back along the wall, slant eyes narrowed. The next moment the man's shadow loomed, bearing straight toward him. He circled wide out through the murk of the rain and came back in, behind him. In the last instant the man turned, saw the board slashing down at him. He had only time to cry out, none at all to dodge the blow. The heavy plank fragment smashed into the side of his head, drove him, stumbling, to his knees. But the damage was done.

Starr whirled, got a knee into the groin of the second shadow, lunging toward him, heard the man scream, saw him go down. Then the third guard was in front of him, firing point-blank, his rifle held hip high. Starr felt the knife slash of the first slug rip across his thigh, that of the second slice through the sleeve of his parka. The third went wild, as the half-breed drove the splintered butt of his board club fully into the rifleman's face. The man fell forward, clawing at his eyes and whimpering in blind pain.

Starr side-stepped him, slid out into Front Street, and was gone. Behind him, as he ran, there was only the sound of the rain now. But he was a long way from home. He knew that and knew that they knew it. They would be after him within minutes, delaying only long enough to warn McClennon at the mercantile. And the pure hell of it was he had only one way to go and they knew that way as well or better than he did.

With the water up like it was, and rising every second, his only chance to leave Nome was to hit for the Snake River bridge, hoping to get across it before it was head-deep under backing tidewater. He kept to the running mud in the middle of Front Street, his long-reaching Indian lope unbroken, his mind leaping ahead to the problem of the crossing.

It had been raining intermittently for a week. All the back-country creeks were out of their banks, the tundra between Nome and the Anvil Creek diggings a quaking morass of sponge mud. The Snake had been cresting and lapping at the floorboards of the suspension span when he had come in over it hours ago. Likely the approach ramps would be under by this time, the tide, driven up the estuary by the onshore wind, already covering the mid-bridge cables. No matter, though. He either got out of town that way, or the Blind Cañon Mine went over to McClennon without a fight.

Luckily one thing was still in his favor. He knew they could not have beaten him to the bridgehead and so he would have only the high water to contend with. The satisfaction of this grim thought lasted less than twenty seconds. Ahead now, the sea wind, sweeping up the Snake, was clearing the estuary so that the rain was thinner there. Visibility was raised to a good fifty or sixty feet, letting him see clearly the motionless clot of men stationed at the bridgehead.

Starr's hand tightened on the club as he slowed his pace to a gliding walk. The men saw him the next moment, but curiously made no move to close in on him. He came up to them, gesturing with the club, his voice slurring harshly: "Get out of my way. I'm going over."

Still they made no move to stop him. "It's the Injun," he heard one of them say, and another answer: "Jesus, yes. I thought McClennon had killed him." Then a third man was moving toward him, calling out: "Good God, man, you can't get across now! She's four feet deep over the middle span!"

Suddenly he knew they were not McClennon's men but only some other miners, like himself, wanting to get across and back upcreek to their own diggings. Yet it was little enough relief. They all knew him. None of them was likely to forget he had gone this way. Plenty of them were sure to let Mc-

Clennon know he had.

He did not answer the man, or the others when they tried to warn him off the span. He stalked through them, plunging into the swirling tide, fighting his way toward the downstream suspension cable. Seizing it, he clung to it, dragging himself hand over hand along it. Twice he went under, the second time so far out from the bankside watchers they could not agree he had come up again and shortly decided that none of them had actually seen him do so. They were still agreeing on the certainty that he had been swept out to sea when McClennon, accompanied by Reno Vail, his chief lieutenant who was called the Faro Kid, and a third man who none of the upcreek miners had ever seen before, panted up through the rain.

"Did ye see him?" the huge Scot challenged them, warning them in the same breath: "We know he had to come this way, lads, so don't be bashful."

"We saw him all right, Mister McClennon," answered the man who had tried to stop Starr. "We did our best to warn him off, but he started on over."

"Started is right," added a second miner. "He sure never finished. We seen him go under about sixty foot out. He ain't come up yet."

McClennon, not replying, pushed past them. He forged out into the flood, bulling his way up the ramp to the main cable piling. There, bracing himself, he peered squintingly along the bellying structure. He was back on the bank the next moment, grinning and stomping the water out of his boots. "Ye watch the tide tomorrow," he told his two companions. "We'll see plenty of bodies spit back up on the beach in the morning. I'm thinking Starr's will be among them."

"Well, I dunno," offered the Faro Kid, a fish-eyed Nevada gambler and fugitive Stateside gunfighter. "They don't always wash back in. I'll give you seven to ten his don't."

"If I was a gambler, ye'd have a bet." McClennon nodded. "But I never bet into a blind hand, as ye know. Still I'm saying he's done for." He turned to the third man, standing a little apart from them, motioning him closer. "What do you think, Tonga? Could he have gotten across?"

The other peered through the rain, studying the bridge and the tidewater now foaming in over the mid-span sag of the cables. He did not answer the Scot's question and

85

did not act as though he intended to. The Faro Kid lifted his thin lip. He did not like McClennon's new bloodhound, slighted no opportunities to let both of them know it.

"God damn you, answer up when a white man asks you a civil question. Did the 'breed get across or didn't he?"

Tonga shrugged his sloping shoulders, turned his blank stare on the Nevadan. "Him part Injun," was all he said.

"And what the hell is that supposed to mean?" demanded the Kid, moving toward him threateningly.

McClennon eased between them. "It's Chinik for anything's possible for an Indian," he told the scowling gunman. "He's saying Starr might have made it safe across. Am I right, mon?" he asked the silent Tonga.

"You no *chock-la-rootin,*" grunted the other.

"Keep translatin', McClennon," gritted the Kid. "If the son-of-a-bitch is insultin' me, I want to know it. If he isn't, there's no point in killin' him. Ammunition costs money."

McClennon flashed his black-browed scowl. "He's only agreeing with me. Said I wasn't lying. Ye take it easy with this Indian now, or ye'll be taking it hard from me, ye understand, Kid? He's made me a million

86

dollars in the past five days but he's still to show me where it's buried." He reached out and patted the expressionless Tonga like he would a sullen but faithful dog.

"Tonga, tonga!" The red man smirked.

That much, that *tonga, tonga* part of it, the Faro Kid understood. "You'll get your lousy whiskey, god damn it!" he snarled. Then, angrily, to McClennon: "I tell you this son-of-a-bitch is sooner or later goin' to snarl our trace lines for good with his infernal drinkin'. You just see if he don't, by God!"

"Don't worry," amended the big Scot softly. "I'll see that he doesn't. Do ye think I'm daft, mon? And him the only one knowing where Starr's mine is? Look, Kid, he's dumb as a dog and that's the way to treat him. Ye pat him and feed him whiskey and he's happy. That's the way we want him, mon, until we're done with him. Quit fretting yerself, lad. It's not like he was a human being, ye know."

The Kid looked at the object of McClennon's self-assurance and could go only so far as to agree with that part of it which said he was not a human being. Tonga Nahahki was a full-blooded Chinik Indian from the Kugruk River country. The Chiniks were a sweet and gentle people. In the

87

summer they tied their no longer useful old men and women in canoes and cut them adrift to go down the river, out into the open sea. In the winter they bound them hand and foot and threw them in the fireless prison of the mucky tent to freeze to death. That was just the way they were — simple, thoughtful, generous to a fault — and Tonga was a prize specimen of their finest manhood. In Chinik his name, Tonga, was the word for the white man's pure grain alcohol, or any other liquid, from good bonded bourbon to barreled coal oil on which a man could get crazy drunk.

Drunk or sober, Tonga Nahahki was a jewel of rare consistency. He could be depended on one day to smile and smirk at a pat on the head, the next, to shove a six-foot seal harpoon through your kidneys for the same kindness. Accordingly it was small wonder that the Faro Kid reserved uneasy judgment on McClennon's confidence in controlling him.

But for his own part the burly Scot had no doubts and only one regret. He should have sent for the murderous heathen much sooner. He had known about Tonga Nahahki's legendary skill as a tracker since the early days up the Yukon. But he had also heard, and more recently, that he had gotten blind drunk on a seal hunt, fallen out of a *umiak,* and been swept under the floe ice up in the Bering Strait. It had been only two weeks ago that a Kotzebue Sound Eskimo had come down from Moran's Station up at Kawalik Lagoon and reported that Tonga was back and living with some Selawik cousins over near the headwaters of Candle Creek, and only five short days ago that the scowling Chinik had shown up in Nome in response to McClennon's message. Now it had been just twenty-four hours ago that he had come back from his stalking of Murrah Starr, to announce that he had found Pushtash Creek and the half-breed's fabulous Blind Cañon Mine.

Grinning over these good thoughts, the hulking owner of the mercantile fetched the hesitant Faro Kid a reassuring clap on the shoulder that would have crippled a yearling grizzly. He swung his fiercely excited gaze back out across the raging Snake.

"Aye mon! Forget the red scut! First thing the fog lifts tomorrow, we'll be setting out for Blind Cañon!" He paused, staring off into the guttering winnow of the rain, up toward Anvil Creek and the out country. The Faro Kid had never heard his heavy voice crack and break and go high like it did then. He did not like the sound of it.

He was beginning not to like the smell and feel of the whole bad business. But he only stepped away from him, watching carefully.

"Angus McClennon's Blind Cañon Mine," the big man croaked hoarsely. He turned away from them to stumble off up Front Street, laughing and muttering wildly to himself as though in all of Nome only Black Angus McClennon was left alive and all the rest of them were as dead and drowned as Murrah Starr.

V

Erin had no trouble getting the gun and cartridges at Bengstrom's. She waited until the store was virtually empty and dealt with a clerk so fresh from the States he still shaved every day to wait on a trade that trimmed its whiskers and changed its underwear twice a year.

True to Starr's prediction the rain was beginning to freeze, laying a slush pack of sleety snow over the mud of Front Street. Her little hand sled, common shopping carrier for Nome's handful of respectable housewives and single women who worked at callings less common than that of the street, attracted little attention. In this latter regard of safe anonymity, the Irish girl's clean reputation and Nome's weird business hours, plus the miserable weather, all conspired to insure her success in getting back to the shack without arousing any curiosity in the few men who stumbled by her on their soggy ways from one source of whiskey to the next.

The town ran open twenty-four hours a day. Nighttime was something that existed only on the battered hands of the saloon and trading companies' wall clocks. It had no meaning for men who were used to seeing the sun set at any time from two o'clock in the afternoon until eleven at night. As for Erin O'Farrell's reputation, she enjoyed that respect unique to the status of unquestioned virtue in a society where every other woman had to take care of eight or ten men and commonly did so at the going rate of sixteen dollars an hour, first come first served.

An orphan, she had lately arrived from Seattle with a hard-drinking uncle in whose doubtful care she had been left. When the latter, within forty-eight hours of landing, had joined his departed brother, her father, via a dispute in Boozer Brown's over the number of aces ordinarily found in a fifty-two card deck, she had gone to work as housekeeper for Father Jacquet, Nome's single pillar of the True Faith. Jacquet, a Pribilof Island Russian with a French name and the unlikely sobriquet of the Teddy Bear, taken from his eccentric habit of wearing a tremendous bearskin coat winter and summer, was a vastly popular figure in the town's early days. Despite his somewhat less than purely sane peculiarities, or perhaps because of them, Nome had taken the erratic Catholic *padre* to her nonsectarian heart. The amorous drunk, Cheechako, or sourdough who would lay a hand or an uncivil word on his shapely ward faced immediately certain, hard-knuckled absolution in Front Street's muddy confessional.

Thus, in the five-minute trudge from Bengstrom's to her shack, the Irish girl was bothered by no more than two or three polite, if wobbly, hat tips and one bourbon-brogued: "Top of the ayv'nin to yez, Erin lass. And whut might the good Fayther be after wantin' yez to fetch this haythin hour of the night? Faith now, but ye're getting' purtier ev'ry gargus day av yer life!"

She got the gun and the wooden case of ammunition into the shack, divided the forty-pound weight of the latter into two gleaming piles, and packed the deadly looking .44 shells in the twin pouches of the wolf dog's pack. He stood quietly for her to do so, making no sound, not even looking at her. When she had finished and tried to offer him some fat salt pork, a delicacy for which he normally would have fought a full team of sled dogs, he only warned her away with a noiseless lift of his black lips.

Straining at the end of his chain, his small, almond-shaped eyes fastened on the door through which Starr had disappeared. He trembled and whined deeply in his throat. It took all her strength to force him back enough to gain the slack to unhook the harness snap of his choke collar. When she had managed it, he leaped past her to the door, the whine an eagerly jaw-chopping growl now.

She unbolted the planks, swung them inward. He went through the opening with a whimpering surge that knocked the latch from her hand, banging the door clear back against the inside wall. Recovering, she had time to see him turn left, directly away from the course Starr had taken and straight up the alley toward the open tundra. Then he was gone.

She fought the door shut against the rising cry of the northwest wind, leaned pantingly against its creaking boards, trying to calm her rapid breathing, collect her confused thoughts. Through a momentary lull in the constant shriek of the gale's building fury, she plainly heard the familiar ticking of the mantel clock across the room. The homely sound jarred her back to reality. It brought her a sudden, frightening sense of where she was and of how swift and late the hour had grown for Erin Eileen O'Farrell. It was two-thirty in the morning of September 27, 1899. She was right squarely in the middle of more trouble than any proper Stateside girl had any reason to think she could ever halfway begin to get herself out of.

You can still read about that storm in the files of the old territorial newspapers. It was the worst early season blow any white man could remember. Nome, built largely within the year of cheap canvas sheeting and packing crate lumber, was literally flattened. When the only slightly lesser darkness of ten o'clock the following morning announced another day, the only buildings to be seen standing through the choking fog that had closed in when the wind died were those precious few constructed of imported material — like Iron Mike McQueen's flophouse, the steel framing for which had been disassembled and floated down the Yukon from the Klondike. Of all the others, no more than another half dozen were still on their pile-driven feet, serving the early morning customers.

Eskimo Town on the Snake's seaward spit was gone. Tent City on the beach was washed away. The invisible surf, still pounding angrily, was weltering the shore with a

95

splintered litter of dories, lighters, barges, and small sailing craft from the outer roadstead. The *Chinook Princess,* a 600-ton tramp from San Francisco, was beached, high and dry, her bow buried halfway through the Seward Company's coal shed. The flimsy shore-boat dockage of the estuary was ground into a match-wood meal and spewed on top of the floating mass of wreckage from the storage sheds and warehouse shacks built along the immediate waterfront. Thirteen bodies were pulled out of the churning surf before noon and the lifting of the fog gave the stunned town its first chance to see where it had formerly stood, and to begin the foul job of mucking out its mud-buried dead and its remaining, tide-battered possessions.

Hundreds of men were already on the beach, working in water to their waists, when Erin, hurrying to get across the Snake River bridge while enough of the fog yet remained to cover her departure, started down Front Street. She was forced to the middle of the road by the hundreds of dull-eyed refugees crowded with their salvaged belongings on the raised boardwalks, or queuing up in pathetic lines in front of the three surviving restaurants. Nearing the mercantile, still standing and apparently undamaged, she slowed instinctively. The next moment she was slipping nervously into the line waiting outside the Flora Dora Chop House.

From the flood-littered barn door of Jernberg's Livery, wedged between the mercantile and the Northern Lights Hotel, a group of scowling horsemen were reining their mounts toward the open center of Front Street's muddy river. Erin watched them as they swung left, toward the bridge, counting seven of them including the bull-shouldered giant in their lead. Of them all, only the slender figure siding the big man sat his saddle as though it were not a painful stranger to him. The others had that hunched, miserable, short-stirruped look common to men who have spent their lives in flat-soled brogans. But awkward rider or not, a poor horse would plow more mud in eight hours than a good man in sixteen. And that ill-assorted posse of seven riders was definitely in a hurry.

Erin's mind struggled to compose the bad picture her blue-green eyes were bringing her. McClennon, of course, she knew, and the wasp-waisted, graceful-riding Faro Kid. Beyond them, there were four Association miners she vaguely remembered having seen from time to time in the mercantile. The hulking, saddle-slumped man riding behind McClennon and the Faro Kid was the stranger — the one she had never seen before. He was, however, obviously an Indian of some sort and, as clearly, from the anthropoid slope of his narrow skull and the Neanderthal sag of his slack jaw, a creature of straight brute intellect. He was as smart, perhaps, as a dog, as dangerous, certainly, as the sullen, furtive-eyed, trained carnival bear of which, for some reason, he at once reminded Erin. She must remember, she told herself, to tell Starr about that Indian. He was such a vicious-looking savage, and so patently out of place in the posse, that his presence must constitute a new and added danger to the half-breed.

She gave them time to get across the bridge, then hurried after them. When she herself had crossed, they were still visible far up the Snake's south bank. But before she had struggled half a mile through the draining litter of the river trail, they had disappeared beyond a distant swell in the tundra and she saw them no more.

The thinning fog still hung low along the river channel. Higher overhead it drifted and swirled to the lift of the wind pushing inland from the beach, shadowing the trail ahead with its depressing midday twilight.

Erin shivered, hesitated, wondered if she dared go on, or if she had the strength to do so, even should she find the courage.

She had, she knew, at least ten miles to cover to reach the rendezvous with Starr. He had not said. Still, one thing remained clear to her. She did not know how far McClennon and his men had to go to reach the half-breed's mine, but mounted as they were and making such swift progress there could lead to only one result. Unless she could somehow communicate with him in time, they would reach it long before Starr did.

She went on, finding the going better as the country grew higher and the northering sun, pale and thin, but a sun nonetheless, appeared briefly. It was the first time she had been this far inland, the first hint she had had of Alaska's sharply defined weather zones. Back at the beach, only a few miles away, the sun was seldom seen from early fall to late spring. Its sickly light was reflected through the coastal murk for a few midday hours up into October. Then even that faint illumination failed and the ghostly snow light of the Arctic winter settled in. After that, the Nome miners set their watches by lamplight until the last of May and the start of the far North's equally uninterrupted three months of strangely nightless summer daylight. But in the back country, although, of course, the sun's autumnal traverse was as brief, the skies were high and clear and dry-aired. The sun could and did make itself known for a few bright hours on either side of high noon.

Erin took heart as its warmth squeezed dry the lichened sponge of the last of the tundra and led her on into the low foothills of the Anvil Creek drainage. Even so, it was after two o'clock when she reached the main settlement, crowding three by the time she had inquired after, found, and started up the Dry Gulch cut-off. But inland or not, that was the limit of the fall daylight. By three-thirty she was moving in the familiar half dark of the long night. Above her, the cañon walls were suddenly rearing 300 and 400 feet high. The few diggings she passed were abandoned for the winter, their owners departed to seek the social delights of Nome until next year's thaw once more unlocked the frozen placer gravels. Again the settlement girl shivered, again thought of the dark-skinned, fierce-eyed man waiting somewhere ahead, and somehow found the strength from that thought to stumble on.

The stillness shortly became a thing to be

felt, and to fear. The only sight was the frost cloud of her labored breathing, the only sound the queasy creak of the scum ice freezing the mud underfoot. A thin scrub of Arctic willow began to appear. It lashed out at her from the darkness, catching and tearing at her trade-blanket Mackinaw. She lost the last sense of time, direction, purpose. She was so weary, when she finally stumbled out into the little clearing, that the sudden looming of Starr's giant figure did not frighten her.

Even the fact that he came up from behind, rather than ahead of her, failed to startle her ragged nerves or impress itself on her numbing mind. She only knew that all at once he was there, his guttural voice soothing her out of the blackness. She remembered thinking she had never heard another sound so deep and dear and welcome in her life. She remembered, too, starting to move toward him, tripping over a willow root in the last step, and beginning to fall. Then his lean arms were reaching to catch her, to take her up, and sweep her in against the blessed warmth of his fox-fur parka, to press her and hold her and keep her there. Past that she did not care, or feel.

VI

Starr carried her less than 100 yards, as tender and awkward about it as though he bore a sleeping child. He moved ahead through the thickening scrub with the long, sure strides of a man who had been there many times before and could trust his feet where his eyes were useless. He found the shallow cave in the base of the bluff where, with Indian caution, he kept a back-trail cache of supplies the year around. He placed her gently upon the blanket already spread over the little cavern's floor of warm, dry sand, left her there, went swiftly about his work. She would be all right; she had only fainted from her nerves letting down on her, as was a white woman's right. Yet he must bring her around as quickly as possible. She must have found out things that he had to know. Had she not, she would not have come so far, so fast. A man in his moccasins could afford no waste of sentimental gratitude.

He got the small, clear-flamed fire of stored dry twigs blazing properly. Taking a smoke-blackened tin can from a cave side ledge, he scooped it full of the soft fresh snow mounding the cavern's mouth, hung it over the fire, sat back to wait for it to boil. He took his first sidelong look at the unconscious girl.

In the rose-shadowed leap of the little fire's shifting light, Erin O'Farrell was something that deserved more than a shy half glance. The half-breed caught his breath, let his slant eyes search her still face. Reaching out, he touched her cheek, the pink lobe of her ear, the full curve of her red mouth, his dark fingers moving like those of a blind man discovering something he had never known before, wondering at its strange, unreal beauty. He brushed the tumbled blackness of her hair, smoothing and patting it wonderingly. His hand leaped back, as her dark lashes trembled slightly. But she was only sighing in her dreamless sleep and he let the hand go back to put the last strand in lingering place. As he brought it away, she stirred restlessly, moving her arm up across her breast, the soft fingers touching his in the motion. Without thinking, he gathered them in, holding them fiercely tight in his lean hand. Slowly he raised her hand to his cheek, pressed its soft palm against his face, held it there a long minute. Then, bringing it away, he put his wide lips to it lingeringly, worshipfully.

Behind him a twig popped, and the first hiss of the beading water broke sharply. Guiltily he put her hand down, covering it with the worn blanket. At the fire, the boiling tin was steaming briskly. From the ledge, he took a small, square can, thumbing its lid off quickly. Carefully he counted the pungent black pekoe into the water, exactly four sparing pinches, not a stem more, and stirred them swiftly. Then he lifted the tin off the fire, set it aside to seep. By the time the fragrant leaves were fully expanded, Erin was opening her eyes.

Hearing her move to sit up, Starr squinted across the fire, nodded solemnly, reached the steaming tin over to her. "Tea," he grunted, dropping his eyes. "See you don't burn yourself. I don't keep any cups here."

She took the tin, holding it a moment to inhale its acrid perfume. She made a little face, smiling across at him. "Tea," she repeated, offering the irrelevancy as people perversely will when bigger talk is tensely expected. "I could never understand what you people up here see in it. What's the matter with coffee?"

"Lots of things, miss." Starr returned her smile hesitantly. "Tea's got it topped ten ways. Packs lighter, lasts longer, boils quicker, hits you faster, goes down better without sugar. What time did you leave town?"

The awkward smile was gone, and so was the time for little talk. Erin gulped at the hot liquid, gasped, felt it burn all the way down. "About noon. I don't think anyone saw me, if that's what's worrying you. It rained right up till ten o'clock or so and the fog was still hanging in when I set out." She smiled again, nodding quickly. "Mister, you're some weather prophet. They're saying it was the worst blow even the Eskimos can remember."

"It figured to be," he agreed. Then, going on, brow knit: "I'm sorry I had to let you come so far in, girl. But when he's playing with the likes of McClennon, a man's got to be good, miss. Real good. There's nobody behind you."

She raised the tin. It was cooler now and she drank deeply, before handing it across to Starr. "There's a good reason for that." She grimaced wryly. "They were ahead of me."

She told him about it then and he heard

her through without interrupting, punctuating the story only with understanding grunts and head bobs after the best Indian fashion. When she had finished, he simply added one more pleased grunt. "Good. They don't worry me too much, once they get outside of town. Back there, they play their rules. Out here, they've got to play mine." There was a slight rasp under the last of it, but his voice immediately gentled again. "We'll rest easy here, for tonight. I'll start you back first thing in the morning. You can make it to town by. . . ."

"Starr!"

There was no mistaking the way her eyes went belatedly wide. He knew she had thought of something she had forgotten to tell him and knew that, whatever it was, it was not good.

He drained the tin, set it on the sand. "Go on," he said. "I'm listening."

"There's something else I meant to warn you about . . . a new man with McClennon . . . an Indian, I think. At least, he. . . ."

It was Starr's turn to interrupt. He did it with his lean hand reaching for the new rifle, his peculiarly blue eyes narrowed to slits. "An Indian, miss?" he repeated softly.

"Yes, I'm sure. He was too big and raw-boned for an Eskimo and I heard a man

106

near me say . . . 'There goes McClennon and his damn', drunk Chinik!' He was a terrible-looking man, Starr. He made me afraid just to look at him. I don't know why."

"I do!" Murrah Starr was already on his feet and moving. "The Chiniks are bad Indians, miss. If McClennon's hired on one of them, you can bet he's picked the worst."

He began sweeping things from the ledge above the fire, making them into a small, flat pack.

"Now you listen to me, girl, and you get it straight the first time through. That Indian makes all the difference. He's bad medicine for me. I got to get out of here right now." He shoved the hand pack inside his parka, got down another blanket for her, went on quickly. "You head back with first light tomorrow. You'll be safe here, warm and dry, for tonight. When you get to town, you get me some things . . . tea, salt, sugar, and a side of bacon, for sure. My pack was left at McClennon's and I didn't get the chance to pick up my supplies. See that you have me some ready at your shack when I come after them."

"All right, all right. . . ." She did not want him to leave, sought anxiously for some way or reason to stay him, and thought she had found it when he began ripping the new

Winchester from its brown-paper wrappings. "Starr, wait! Where's the dog? What about Smoke? The bullets . . . ?"

Bullets, he thought, and his dark grin flicked and was gone. There was a settlement woman for you. Calling cartridges bullets. Well, the less she knew or ever found out about such things, the better for both of them.

"He's where he ought to be," he answered her. "Downtrail, watching out." He stepped to the mouth of the cave, whistled once. It was a low, shivery sound, as thin and distant as a wolf howl lost in the winter wind. Moments later the wolf dog appeared outside the cave, his yellow eyes burning green in the fire's faint light. He whined once, waved his plumed tail, spread his blunt jaws in an obvious wolf grin of gladness at being with Starr again.

As he moved to follow the latter back in under the bluff, Erin reached out impulsively to pat the ugly head. Starr's hand snaked out and nailed her wrist, as the stub ears flattened and the long fangs came uncovered.

"Don't ever try to touch him . . . or me . . . when we're together," he warned harshly. "It's the only thing I've never been able to teach him. Been that way ever since

I took him out of that trap. It's been four years but it seems he still figures he owes me one." The half-breed paused, his blue eyes driving into the girl's. "Likely the same as I figure I owe you, miss."

With the words he hunched his shoulders to settle the parka, picked up the new gun, turned to go. His deep voice was still strangely soft.

"Be careful, girl. I'll never forget you. You're all the human friend I've ever had."

She made no effort to hide the brimming tears. "Oh Starr, Starr! When will I see you again . . . ?" It was not so much a question as an outright, lonely plea. With it, she moved toward him, slender arms reaching hungrily.

He stepped back, snarling at the wolf dog to stay away from her. When he spoke to her, the old guttural thickness was back in his slurring speech, and she knew the fleeting moment of his softness was gone.

"When will you see me again, miss?" he repeated cynically. "Next spring, when the ice goes out of the Snake. You stand on the bridge then and look careful at what bobs past and washes out to sea. Mine'll be the body that comes by, belly down, with the bullet holes in the back of the head."

After that, it was the same for her as it

had been at the shack. One minute he was there, talking to her, the next she was staring at nothing but the empty dark, and her low cry was being answered only by the muttering prowl of the night wind.

She was left alone, frighteningly, completely alone. And her only thought was the desperate one that formed even as the slight sounds of the half-breed's footsteps were still dying away.

She did not know how far he had yet to go to reach his mine, or how much of a start McClennon had on him by this time. But one thing was still as certain as Erin O'Farrell was standing there in that lonely cave entrance. When he reached his barren shack on the distant headwaters of Pushtash Creek, Black Angus McClennon and his men would be waiting to murder Murrah Starr.

VII

Tonga had said it was a two-day walk to the Pushtash Creek country. Not being a horseman he had been unable to translate that into mounted miles, so in effect McClennon had no exact idea of how far it was to Starr's mine. Being a graduate *cum sourdough laude* of the University of the Upper Yukon, he should have been able to figure it. But like his earlier counterpart in the American West, the far Northern frontiersman seldom bothered to acquire any real knowledge of Indians. Accordingly the bad-tempered Scot did not realize that when a nomad Chinik, who could walk a caribou herd down, shrugged a term like "two-day-easy" he was indicating a foot pace it would take a good horse to equal. But he found out.

It was edging toward the three o'clock twilight of the second day when the sullen Indian halted his horse, pointed up a sparsely timbered draw, and grunted: "House up there *kill-a-muck* way."

"What the hell did he say?" groused the Faro Kid, pulling his own mount in and glowering the question at McClennon.

The latter returned his glare. It had been a bad trail up, through country rougher than a Pribilof Russian's beard. Tempers were growing trigger touchy. "He says Starr's shack is just up yonder gulch, mon. *Kill-a-muck*'s their word for quick."

"It's a good word." The spare gunman nodded. "I'll remember it. It's the way I'm goin' to kill that son-of-a-bitch someday."

If the Indian understood him, he gave no sign. "Go now," he said. "Sleep in little house. Him warm."

"Well, you've got that right anyhow," admitted the thin Nevadan. "It's turnin' colder than a banker's stare."

"Yeah, and it's coming on to snow again sure as a Siwash squaw smells bad," growled one of the others. "Let's get the hell up there and move in."

"We're got," said the Faro Kid, and turned his mount to follow Tonga's and McClennon's.

It was full dark, with the wind rising and the first sharp flakes stinging in out of the north, when they halted the lathered horses

112

in front of Starr's bleak hut and gave it a long, hard look. It was a typical structure of its outcreek kind, a jerrybuilt patchwork of scrub timbers, powder-box boards, settlement canvas, and corrugated sheet iron. It had one oilskin window, a leather-hinged plank door, a weirdly staggering black stovepipe. There was no apparent sign of life in or about it.

"What do ye think, Tonga mon?" McClennon stayed on his horse awaiting the Indian's opinion. Behind him the others crowded their mounts forward impatiently, hunching their backs against the whip and cut of the wind.

"Me no like. Too quiet. Him too dark for see tracks."

"What the hell does that mean?" demanded the Faro Kid. "You think maybe he's beat us here? He might be in there?"

"Him part Injun. Me no like."

"Oh, hell, you're crazy, you dumb red ape! If he ain't slept since leavin' Nome, he still couldn't make it here six hours short of noon tomorrow!"

"Me crazy," agreed the Chinik. "You smart. You go in, me stay out here."

McClennon shoved his horse between them, heavy voice rasping. "Listen, Tonga mon, talk straight, ye savvy?" He reached out in the dark, giving him the good dog pat on the shoulder. "Now then, is he in there or not? What are ye trying to say, mon?"

The Chinik looked at him, shrugged blankly. "Me say me no like."

McClennon swung his mount toward the others. "It's no use, boys," he told them. "It's like trying to put a dull pick through January gravel. He seems to have an idea the 'breed may have beat us here, near as I can gather. What do ye think?"

"Shure and I'm thinkin' it's colder than a Husky's butt in a snow bank." Big Tim Rafferty, one of the Association miners, shivered. "Yez kin set out here and argue with that blockhead Injun scut all winter if yez like. I'm goin' in."

"Same here," grumbled another of the men. "My insides are shaking worse'n a back-home boy with his hand on the schoolmarm's leg. Besides, where's the worry? The 'breed ain't got his gun, nor even his knife no more."

"All right," grated McClennon. "What do ye say, Kid?"

"She's unanimous," vouchsafed the transplanted son of the southern cow country. "Furthermore, if we don't get these sweated-up ponies in outen this wind we're

114

goin' to be walkin' back home. There's some sort of lean-to shed yonder there past the shack. I'll put 'em up."

"Aye." The huge Scot nodded. "Tonga will help ye." He grunted a couple of Chinik words to the latter, turned back to the men. "Come on, lads. The rest of us will go in and make a light and get a good blaze started."

The Faro Kid gathered in the looped reins of the nearest horses, started for the shed. Tonga followed behind him with the other horses.

"Faith now, and it's blacker than a Protestant's heart in here!" complained Big Tim, inside the shack, feeling his way along the wall. "Strike a light there, will yez, Frenchy? How the divil do you expect a man to find the bloody lamp?"

"Leave him find it in the dark, Jules," one of the others said nervously. "Maybe he'll bust a leg and we can shoot him."

"Ah, now," breathed the Irishman. "There's a bright lad, Lucas. Yez keep that up and ye'll spare the Association the expense of layin' out yer haythin carcass."

"Don't let him swarm you under, Lucas," comforted a third of the edgy miners. "It ain't for nothing they're knowed as flannel mouths. If him and his bog-trotting kind

115

could bite as hard as they blow, there wouldn't be a lodge saving the Loyal Sons of Saint Patrick north of the Canadian line."

"Shure, now, Jackson lad, the Association is makin' money hand over fist this night," sighed Big Tim. "That's two funerals will never come out of the blessed buryin' fund. Yez goin' to strike that light, Frenchy dear? Or will yez be after savin' Father Jacquet the trubble of givin' yez absolution when ye're no longer listenin'?"

Armand "Dirty Jules" Ladoux, careful to put his replying insult in safe Canuck French, complied forthwith. The sulphur match scraped the log wall, sputtered, flared smokily. In the brief instant of its life several things happened.

Big Tim Rafferty never found his lamp. Instead, and for the benefit of future generations of Raffertys, he found his voice. "Jesus Murphy!" bellowed the Irishman, wild-eyed. "Look out . . . !"

With his warning roar he was diving for the floor, and the cabin-close thunder of Starr's Winchester was rocking the flimsy shack to its willow underpinnings. The first five shots were gotten off in the time it took Ladoux to drop the match and grab his guts. The next two came while the match was falling. The last one ricocheted crazily through the blind darkness, after the match had struck the floor and been snuffed out. The next, and final, sounds the white posse heard were the crash of the shattering window frame, as Starr's leaping body hurtled through it, a sudden, deep-throated burst of wolf snarling outside, and a single, agonized human scream followed by the bucking roar of the Faro Kid's twin .44s. Then there were only the tooth-gritting groans of the wounded inside the shack and the Kid's livid curses continuing outside of it.

McClennon got up from the floor where Big Tim's wild dive had knocked him. He struck another match, found, lit, and turned up the lamp. Then he looked around him. The half-breed's shack was a shambles.

Jackson and Lucas were dead, Ladoux dying, Rafferty, with a nasty flesh wound furrowing his left arm from wrist to shoulder, was down and bleeding like a slaughterhouse beef. McClennon himself was unhit and unharmed except for an ugly four-inch gash where his forehead had smashed against Starr's woodbox in falling. He was still standing there, swaying from the double shock of that plus the *abattoir* of the half-breed's ambush when the Faro Kid staggered in, supporting the stricken Tonga Na-hahki.

The Nevada gambler was unmarked but his companion was as bloody as the cabin floor under Big Tim Rafferty. The third jolt of seeing his precious Chinik bloodhound torn up cleared McClennon's dazed eyes.

"My God, mon!" he rasped to the Kid. "What happened to him?"

"The god-damn' wolf!" snapped the latter. "We heard the firin' in here and come a-runnin'. Halfway from the shed, somebody come flyin' through the window. He hit the ground hard and didn't get right up. Your Injun, here, split off and headed in on him."

"Starr!" snarled McClennon. "He was in here. Opened up when we struck a light."

"Figures." The Faro Kid nodded. "Your Chinik didn't get nowheres near him outside, though. The wolf come out from under the shack and hit him chest high. The Injun heard him comin' in time to get his arms up apparently. Otherwise, he'd still be out there. Jesus, that's a big wolf. Looked the size of a weanlin' calf in that dark out there."

McClennon, staring at the silent Chinik brave, came as close as his unfeeling kind can to being afraid. From beaded collar to belted sash, the Indian's buckskin hunting shirt hung in ribbons. The foot-long slashes of the wolf dog's tushes, sunk to their bared

118

gums, had laid the dark chest beneath it opcn to the sickening white of the exposed breast bones.

"He'd have finished him clean off," muttered the Faro Kid in still awed tones, "but for the half-breed. He jumped up and called him off, just as I was movin' in and gettin' my guns loose. I swear to Christ they was talkin' wolf back and forth. Leastways, the god-damn' critter left go of the Injun and follered the 'breed off like a buggy-whipped hound. They took off downcrick. You figure it, mister. It's one too many for me."

"I am figuring it, mon!" The richening burr of his Celtic forebears announced the return of McClennon's mind to its normal channel of deadly slow cunning. "Aye, ye just wait till we get back to Nome with these dead lads draped across their horses! We'll have every honest miner in the Association fighting for places in the next posse. Aye, and that's but the half of it, too. LaMont will have to get out a murder warrant, setting everything up dead legal." He broke off, nodding softly across the cabin toward the empty window frame. "Aye, Starr mon, ye've done it this time. Ye've fixed yerself for certain sure, lad."

"Certain shure is it now?" inquired Big Tim pithily. The Irishman nodded the observation with his right hand clamping his left wrist to strangle the pump of the torn artery. "Faith, and it looks to Missus Rafferty's bye Timothy as though 'tis us has bin fixed. The saints be praised, 'tis nothin' but the pure luck of the Irish and Frenchy droppin' the bloody match that the rest of us ain't arguin' with the divil this same minute."

"Honest to God, Rafferty," drawled the Faro Kid wonderingly, "you'll outtalk the preacher at your own funeral. Christ, don't you never run down?" He bent over him quickly, his examination that of a qualified expert on gunshot wounds. "Hold still. Leave me look at that damn' arm."

"Tie it off for him," ordered McClennon behind them. "I'll get the Indian's shirt off."

"How about Frenchy?" countered the Kid over his shoulder.

The big Scot moved across the room. Looking down, he put the toe of his sealskin boot under the Canuck's side, pushed him a quarter turn over, pulled the boot away. Ladoux's body flopped back, collapsing like a drawn chicken's.

"He's dead. Get over here under the light, Tonga."

They bound the two men with strips from Starr's supply of patching canvas, plastering their wounds shut with dry flour after first scrubbing them out with clean snow. They took care of Big Tim first, needing him to help with what they had to do for Tonga. The Indian had been dog bitten. There was no way but to burn out the wound.

They stretched the Indian flat on his back on Starr's crude table, under the lamp that hung from the shack's low center pole. McClennon pinned his arms; the Kid bulldogged his feet. Big Tim got the battered can of lighting kerosene from back of the stove, poured the long, shallow wound full of the yellow coal oil.

"Hold yer breath, damn yez!" He glared at the Indian. "Ye're spillin' it over the edges!" Tonga nodded, freezing the rise and fall of his broad chest. The Irishman refilled the wound, struck the match. "Cinch 'im tight, now, byes!" he gritted, and touched the match to the reddening oil.

Tonga's eyes bulged. He made a single brute sound and bit clear through the strap of dog harness McClennon had set between his teeth. Then the main searing flare of the burning oil died back. Big Tim beat out its lingering edges with an empty flour sack and it was over. They bandaged him quickly, lacing the canvas skin-tight with Starr's dog harness, mending awl, and waxed thread.

When they were through, they stepped away from the table, and the Chinik sat up. He swung his feet to the floor, stood up, his dark face gray with pain. Straightening himself, he looked at McClennon, and his first words were: "We kill him now." With the expressionless grunt he stalked past them, out the door into the night.

Angus McClennon nodded softly after him, picked up the dead body of Jules Ladoux, and followed him out.

VIII

Immediately upon his return, McClennon filed a protest claim against the Pushtash Creek location, re-recording it in his own name, and furnishing for the first time an exact description of its long-secret whereabouts. By way of quasi-legal excuse he glibly quoted the abortive resolution that had originally brought Starr into Nome and that McClennon had earlier been instrumental in persuading the Miners Association to adopt. He now shrewdly guessed that the organization would accept the resolution as interim law, pending receipt of Washington's expected negative ruling.

The wily Scot was gambling on borrowed time and on the validity of the old mining camp law of possession. He understood that clearly and knew that his best chance of getting the Blind Cañon Mine was to establish that possession before the government's writ of refusal could arrive. In this regard the odds favored him heavily.

Rank-and-file-wise, the Miners Association of Nome was not corrupt, did a good general job of policing its members in the wild town on the beach at Norton Sound. But like a hundred similar vigilante labor groups before and since, it was dominated from the top by its elected officials. If those officials were entirely able and honest, the various gold-strike settlement associations left fine records. If they were not, a miner's life was worth no more, nor less, than the real or rumored value of his claim. And in Nome, that second year, the elected head of the Miners Association was Angus Colloch McClennon.

During the brief history of the bonanza at the mouth of the Snake, dozens of claims had already been filed upon by as many as ten different men. The legal owner became simply the last one of those ten still alive and standing off the eleventh with the most convincing argument of jurisprudence locally available — more often than not a late model Winchester rifle. Under Norton Sound law, possession was not nine points, it was all ten and then some. As to Murrah Starr's Blind Cañon strike, Angus McClennon according to the best evidence outstanding — his own — had established due cause and reason to file a dispute claimer on the Pushtash Creck diggings.

The next step was to convince the Association of that fact, thus insuring the success of his plan to see that the half-breed spent the rest of the winter under the Snake River ice — legally. Toward that admirable end, McClennon now moved swiftly. Back in Nome and facing a carefully chosen rump session, he told a simple, clearly forthright story.

He and his group had been in the back country innocently running out a report of some rich gravel color brought in by Tonga Nahahki, his newly hired Chinik Indian guide. He and his little company had been in an understandable hurry. Any old Yukon hand would see that and agree with it. Naturally. The season was late, the placers would soon be frozen in, past the possibility of exploration. So much for his group's honest reason for being so far up the creeks. Now for the terrible atrocity that had forced them to return.

The early snowstorm, the same one still piling up outside as he talked to his outraged fellow members, had caught them in the open. Seeking shelter, they had stumbled by accident upon the half-breed's camp. They had, of course and unthinkingly, entered his shack to take refuge as wilderness law permitted. Imagine their horror and profound shock when the murderous half-breed, hidden in the darkest recess of the apparently abandoned dwelling, opened fire on them without warning. It was truly a monstrous crime and one that must not go unpunished.

McClennon had a true Highlander's moody flair for the dramatic. He exercised it overtime in painting the black portrait of Starr's wanton depravity for his angry listeners. His lurid story, coupled with the eloquent testimony of the packed-in bodies of Ladoux as well as those Lucas and Jackson, both popular charter members, was all the Association required. A hundred indignant miners at once volunteered to go back with honest Angus to help him serve the murder warrant a reluctant U.S. Marshal LaMont was forthwith forced to issue.

But the canny owner of the mercantile played out his rigged hand with solid Celtic caution. There must be no hint of mob action, he pleaded selflessly. Let there be impartial justice, no matter the enormity of the half-breed's offense. Just let McClennon go up the creeks with a small, duly constituted posse. He would be willing to spare himself for the odious task and felt that someone of his eminent stature in the community should head the expedition to guarantee both the ends of uninflamed justice and the good sense of the Association.

Forty-eight hours later, accompanied by twenty of the most highly respected members, plus both of LaMont's deputies and the warrant for Murrah Starr, he set out for the Pushtash. His was clearly a lawful posse, from the carefully insisted upon presence of the deputy marshals, and had Starr had the good sense to surrender to it he might have lived out the winter in Nome's jail, hence, partially at least, embarrassing McClennon's murderous move. But the big Scot knew his man. He accepted that calculated risk and got cleanly away with it.

The half-breed was not at the shack, nor did he come near it in the three fruitless, freezing cold days the posse camped along the Upper Pushtash waiting for him to do so. When, late the following Saturday night, the frustrated manhunters returned to Nome, Angus McClennon's plan was working exactly on deadly schedule. He had staged a patently legitimate attempt to serve the ends of territorial justice. The attempt had failed, as he knew it must, thus paving the way for putting subsequent law into bolder, less binding hands — Angus Mc-Clennon's for present hard instance. He was now free to go after the half-breed in his own sweet way and time and with his own judiciously hired men.

Yet ten minutes after he got back to Nome that Saturday night, McClennon knew that his way was not going to be so sweet, or his time so selective. He was going to have to move right now, if not sooner. Word of his recent address to his handpicked rump session of the Association had seeped out to the uninvited members, and, through their angry complaints, to certain non-members. There were by now plenty of the foreign-born claim owners beginning to share Mur-rah Starr's uneasiness over the Association's "anti-square-head" resolution. A "square head" was Nome's deprecating term for any foreigner. At first no one had really believed it could work, or that any serious attempt would be undertaken to make it work. This was an United States Territory. The United States was not like the homelands from which so many of them had come. It had laws to protect the innocent and those laws were not just words on paper. But after Mc-Clennon's announced filing on Starr's claim, with the half-breed presumably still alive and in technical possession of his

128

rights, murder warrant or not, more than a few of the non-American miners began to worry out loud — loud enough, in fact, to be heard by Colonel Pruett Johnson at nearby Fort Michael.

McClennon was still getting out of his parka in his room behind the mercantile when the Faro Kid lounged in with the latest news. Front Street was full of bluecoats. Patrols were right then being stationed up and down the main stem from the tundra to the tidewater. Johnson had just called an Association meeting, requesting the attendance of all interested members and ordering that of Mr. Angus Colloch McClennon.

The air in the shack turned blue as a badman's beard for the next fifteen seconds. The noncommittal Kid was offering himself ten-to-one that McClennon was going to break every blood vessel in his bear-sized body before he got through. But shortly the big Scot calmed down, growled back into his parka, and stomped off down Front Street.

He was back in half an hour, grinding the spoiled meat of the hearing between his stumpy teeth. But curse, stomp, rage, snarl, and snap at it as he would, the taste of that meat grew no sweeter. In the end he had to

129

spit it out and admit that legally he was licked.

As of 10:00p.m. the night of October 8, 1899, Nome was under martial law. According to Colonel Pruett Henry Johnson, U.S.A., it was going to stay that way until the final writ of refusal on the Association's anti-foreigner petition came through from Washington, D.C.

Thinking furiously, McClennon knew he was down to his last five cards. It was, however, a hand he had played before and could play again. Of course, it was a shame the Army had gotten in the way of his legal arrangement for murdering Starr and too bad, additionally, that the presence of the troops was bluffing the boys in the Association out of backing him on the resolution gamble. But if the situation now called for a man who could go after the half-breed the good old-fashioned way, he knew just the man. His name was Black Angus McClennon and, if it was the last act of his claim-jumping life, he was going to hunt down that blue-eyed, half-Indian bastard and this time make dead sure of his own presently doubtful title to the fabulous Blind Cañon Mine.

Within the hour of Colonel Johnson's proclamation, McClennon was calmly briefing the hard-eyed members of his last posse. There were only ten of them, including himself, the Faro Kid, Big Tim Rafferty, and Tonga Nahahki. Every man was sworn to secrecy and promised a big fraction of Starr's original claim should the present adventure achieve its lethal aim of a clear title for Angus McClennon. Since the departure of such a sizable group might be noticed, a story was prepared to the effect that McClennon, as head of the Miners Association and in the higher interests of the law that association had been founded to uphold, was going out on his courageous own to bring Starr in for trial on the murder warrant.

The big Scot, as organizer of the effort, would furnish all supplies and stand any expense incurred therein. They would pack into the Pushtash by dog sled, set up their base camp at Starr's shack, work out from there on snowshoes. The prospects looked very good.

The big freeze was coming fast now. Chances were, the last ship for the States would sail within the week. The offshore ice was already starting to form, would probably have the Sound sealed in solid before they got back. After that, no word from the outside, no government writs or anything else, would reach Nome until the 1900 breakup. Were there any questions?

There were a few. McClennon answered them tersely. The last wash of understanding head nods went around the listening circle shortly before midnight, and the meeting at once adjourned to the darkened mercantile to outfit and load the three sleds that would be used.

The snow was spitting in across the Sound through the bared teeth of a Bering Straits gale, when they set out an hour later. They went silently up Front Street, turning right into the first alley leading out to the open tundra. It was exactly 1:00a.m. by the rusted chimes of her mantel clock when a restlessly turning Erin O'Farrell, ten days returned from her Dry Gulch Cañon rendezvous with Starr and with no intervening word whatever from the desperate half-breed, heard the frosty creak of wooden-shod runners and the panting whine of eager sled dogs passing outside her shanty window. The muffled sounds brought the frightened girl bolt upright in the lonely blackness of her tiny bunk.

She reached the window as the first of the three dog teams, already past the shack, was heading out across the tundra. But the gray snow light let her see clearly the gaunt, slope-shouldered silhouette of the man driving it. There was no mistaking the brutish form of Tonga Nahahki. The second driver's figure was as familiar, McClennon's, and the third was that of the thin, easy-drawling card dealer they called the Faro Kid. Behind them came the single file of men on snowshoes, following in the narrow track of the dog sleds. Of these she recognized only the bulky man in the lead, a jovial, well-liked Association miner named Timothy Rafferty.

Watching the last of the swiftly plodding line disappear into the snowy whirl of the tundra wind, the settlement girl's eyes widened suddenly. Familiar and frightening as those passing forms had been, there was something still more familiar and, somehow, even more frightening about the lean shadow that drifted up the alley behind them and that, in the next tense moment, was turning to slide noiselessly toward her door. It was Murrah Starr.

IX

She let him in, standing back apprehensively as the wolf dog, in response to one of the half-breed's strange-tongued orders, appeared out of the snow-filled darkness and slunk into the shack behind him.

"I wish you'd talk English to that dog!" she blurted. "It gives a body the creeps the way you two growl back and forth!"

A little of the low-voiced indignation was honest Irish showing through. Most of it was pure bluff, put on to cover the nasty jump his sudden appearance had given her pulse. Starr, sensing her upset, sounded oddly pleased.

"It wouldn't do any good, miss." His teeth were so white she could see the grin flash even in the cabin's darkness. "He doesn't savvy a word of English, saving his name. Even there he answers better to *Sotaju*."

"To what?" she delayed, wanting time to think and to calm the bad excitement his nearness had stirred within her from the beginning.

"*Sotaju,*" he repeated slurringly. "That's Smoke in my mother's tongue."

"Thanks," she said deprecatingly. "Maybe next time he tries to take my hand off, I can talk him out of it in his own language."

"Don't try it," advised Starr. "Leastways, not until you've learned a little more of it." The rare vein of iron humor in his voice thinned out abruptly. "Did you get the things I asked you to, miss? Tea, sugar, beans, flour, bacon . . . ?"

"All but the bacon," she interrupted nervously. "There's a shortage and I didn't have enough money left." She added defensively: "Your dust all went for the gun and the bullets."

The half-breed laughed. At least it sounded to the girl as though he meant it be a laugh. "There's a white man's moral in that some place," he said. "An Indian with a million dollars can't buy a slab of side meat." He kicked out of his snowshoes, knocked the clinging trail ice from them, set them carefully against the wall with the precious rifle. "You got a spare blanket handy?"

"Yes. What for?"

"Fetch it."

She brought him the blanket, waiting restlessly while he hung it over the rattling windowpanes and forced its edges carefully under the jut of the rough frame, all around.

"All right. Let's have the light now. Trim it as low as you can."

She found and lit the lamp, turning down its corded wick until the yellow flame smoked thinly. Moving swiftly from the window, Starr took it from her. As quickly he set it behind the stove, placing it so that its feeble light was cut yet further. Still moving easily but with cat-deft speed, he opened the stovepipe damper, putting a sucking draft to the banked morning fire. When the sleeping coals began to yawn and push back their powdery blanket of gray night ash, he reset the damper, and armed out of his parka. Then, in turn, he toed out of his knee-length sealskin snow boots, and faced her, his lean back hunched gratefully to the rising warmth.

It was the first time the girl had seen him out of the shrouding bulk of the fox-fur parka and the only time she had seen him without the disfiguring welts of McClennon's brutal beating puffing his dark face.

As her eyes adjusted to the dim light, he remained motionless before the stove, giving her time for a good long look, while he took one himself. The Irish girl saw a man who must certainly, even standing in the thin soles of his soft-tanned camp moccasins, shade six feet. In his grease-blackened Indian buckskins he looked as spare and grim and deadly straight as the hard-polished haft of a Selawick sealing harpoon. But it was his face that held her eyes finally. They had called him a half-breed, part unnamed white, part unknown Indian. His skin was the color of Cordovan boot leather. The bony structure beneath it was as savagely cut and shadowed as a Kotzebue ivory carving. His hair, shoulder long and coarse as a bear's, reached back from his low forehead in a shaggy blue-black mane. His nose and mouth were out of an aboriginal skin painting, the former as big and cruelly bridged as a fish-hawk's beak, the latter as warm and pleasant and re-assuring as a knife slash. Only in his strangely blue eyes was there any hopeful hint of a possible white heritage, and even that slight chance was hedged by the high-boned Mongol slant with which their peculiar blue brilliance was set into the copper-dark mounting of his alien face.

Looking at him now, Erin O'Farrell shivered uncontrollably and was suddenly not quite so sure of her impulsive friendship for the hunted outcast of the Pushtash. She was as suddenly, if belatedly, aware of the fact she was standing in front of him in a flimsy nightgown. She hesitated, somehow not daring to move while he was watching her.

For his part, Murrah Starr was shivering, too, but not from fear or confusion. Staring unblinkingly at the flushed white girl, he was fighting down the old wild cry of the south wind in the spruce tops, driving out of his darkening thoughts the naked animal hunger of the far and lonely night fires. To say something, anything, to break the danger he could sense growing in the eye-locked stillness between himself and the lightly clad settlement woman, he forced the second iron-hard grin. "Along about here," he told her, the deepening slur of his words giving the lie to their attempted lightness, "my people would be saying *ho-hah-hee.*"

"*Ho-hah-hee?* What does that mean, Starr?"

She hoped desperately that the forced confidence of her return smile and the impersonally familiar use of his name would take his eyes off of her, give her the chance to move naturally for a blanket from the bunk with which to cover herself.

He nodded deliberately, letting her know he saw past her too bright question. But at

138

the same time he gracefully obeyed its urgent intention, as though he could read her mind as easily as her red lips. He swung quietly around, spreading his dark hands to the hissing warmth of the stove, purposely turning the lean square of his shoulders to the grateful girl.

"It means welcome to my teepee," he said evenly. "We usually boil a little tea along with it."

She came to the stove, the blanket pinned tightly about her. "All right, I owe you a cup. What can I fix you with it? I've got yesterday's pan bread and just a bit of bacon left."

"No thanks, miss. We've eaten. Smoke jumped a snowshoe hare out on the tundra a few minutes back. We held up to make use of it."

She got water from the bucket, set a small saucepan on the front lid. "You took quite a chance, didn't you? Building a fire so close to town. I mean . . . knowing they were after you . . . and *why* they were after you."

"I didn't say anything about building a fire."

"But you said. . . ."

"Indian style, miss. Right off the rabbit. Warm, you might say, but not cooked."

Again the little shiver ran through her. She

139

stole a glance at him, noticing for the first time the smears on his extended hands, where the stove light struck them. In one place a few of the short white hairs were still embedded in the drying crust under his fingernails. His slant eyes trapped hers to the furtive inspection.

"Sorry, miss. I'll wash up for tea."

"Don't bother!" She was short with it, drawn beyond the edge of her fear of him by the cynical rebuke in his blunt apology. "At least, it's only rabbit blood this time!"

He wheeled on her, his anger real now. "That's twice I don't like the way you said something. A minute ago it was why somebody was after me. Now it's rabbit's blood this time. Say what you mean, miss. I don't like riddles."

Whatever it might be, Erin knew, the half-breed was no liar. "Don't you know?" she asked, shaking her head slowly.

"Not till you tell me."

She told him then, all that had happened in Nome since she had given him the rifle in Dry Gulch Cañon, concluding bitterly: "That's the blood I mean is on your hands! You killed three men in that shack up there. You're a murderer, Murrah Starr!"

The saucepan broke into a boil. Starr got up, pinched the tea into it. He brought it

140

back to the table, with the cups, sat back down across from her. The silence pressed in. He continued to stare at her, his intensely blue eyes searching her drawn face, his stillness somehow far more accusing than her angry words.

At last he spoke, the pure surprise of his soft question unnerving her. "You still want to help me, girl?" was all he said.

It was a simple thing to ask. A frightening, dangerously complicated thing to answer. And Erin O'Farrell had no answer ready for it. It was easy to be afraid of him when he slunk in out of the morning blackness as he just had. Or when you saw him the way he had looked, staring at what was under your nightgown. It was no trick at all to shudder and tell yourself he was a three-time murderer, from ambush and in cold blood, and that you never wanted or dared to see him again in your soft little life — when he was somewhere far out across the tundra. But when he was sitting across a two-foot table from you in the toasty-warm lamplight of a cabin, with nothing between you and the exciting, lean look of him save your good girl's conscience and a hastily pinned trade blanket, it was quite another, confusingly passionate matter.

Still, where she might not know herself,

and certainly did not know the strange dark man she had so impulsively befriended, Erin knew right from wrong. The half-breed was a brutal murderer, legally wanted by the only constituted law in Alaska Territory. No decent woman, knowing what Erin did about him and his monstrous crime, could move another moral step with him along the wicked path upon which he had led her. But as she opened her mouth to tell him so, his sinewy hand shot across the table, pinning hers to the rough boards.

"Miss, don't say it. Wait."

He took his hand away, pushed back from the table, went again to the stove, and stood with his back to her. When he spoke, his deep voice was as gentle as the lisp of the snow against the blanketed windowpanes. And to the following, wind-still quiet, punctuated only by the peaceful mutter of the drowsing coals, Murrah Starr told his story.

X

"White men often lie, miss," he began. "But when they say I am an Indian, their tongues are straight. My mother was a full-blood Oglala Sioux. My father was a white man I never saw. He was a renegade, miss, a traitor . . . fought with my mother's people against his own color, against Custer and the Seventh Cavalry at the Little Big Horn. He was a full war chief of the Oglala, an adopted blood brother of Tashunka Witko, Crazy Horse himself. But when Tashunka took our people in to surrender to the Pony Soldiers after the big fight along the Greasy Grass, my father did not go with him.

"I was born, and my mother died, during that battle with Custer. Sitting Bull, miss, was my godfather. He took me with him when he fled with his Hunkpapa Sioux to Canada. I was raised there, in a teepee, miss. I never saw a white man, other than the Red Coats who came once a year to see that we kept the peace, until many years later when Sitting Bull led our people back to the States.

"I went to the white man's school then, there in Dakota. I learned what I know of his harsh language, and of the bad way that he thinks of things and does them. Those were unhappy years for me. The only life I knew was the Indian life. The only land I could remember was the Northland. This snow and cold and clear far sky up here. These wind-sharp sunny days and long-quiet lonely nights. This smell of drifting teepee smoke and this wild sound the south wind makes when it talks, soft and crazy, through the spruce tops."

He stopped and for a breath-held moment she thought he had finished. Then, shortly, the strangely musical rhythm of his oddly slurred speech began again, and she fell once more under its fascination.

"When Tall Bear took a small band of young men and left that reservation down there, I went with him. The Pony Soldiers caught us near the borderline. Tall Bear died in the fighting. So did all the others. I, alone, got away and escaped across the line.

"I was bad hurt. My left leg was like a log dragging behind me. The bullet had broken the bone and I knew that I was going to die, too. But I had only one thought . . . to come back to the pines and the snow once more before I passed over into my people's Land of the Shadows.

"Somehow, I got there . . . back to my home. But the teepees were gone. There was nothing in our camp but the old fire spots and the empty circles in the brown earth where the lodges had been. I lay down there, in that bare place where Sitting Bull's lodge had stood. I was ready to die and wanted to die. With all my people gone, with only the white men left to live among, I was better dead. I was the last Sioux. . . ."

There was the long pause again after that. Yet this time Erin knew he had not finished, waited tensely for him to do so.

"A funny thing happened then." His vibrant voice faded, as a man's will when it is traveling far back along a poignantly remembered trail. "I thought I heard a dog whine, in that dead place where there could be no dogs. I looked up from where I lay and saw that it was a wolf. A young wolf, caught in a rusted trap set long ago and forgotten through the years by one of our hunters. He was coming toward me, crawling on his belly and dragging the trap log and heavy chain behind him. He came clear up to me and laid down close by me. He looked at me, whining and wagging his tail as you've seen him do a dozen times.

"I thought all sorts of crazy things . . . that I was dreaming or, more likely, dead. That this was a spirit wolf, sent by the Great Spirit to guide me to the Land of the Shadows. Still, I got up and let him out of the trap. I even splinted his broken leg the best I could. When I was through, he licked my hand and limped off a ways. I kept thinking he would go away soon. But he didn't. He just kept standing there, whining and wagging his tail. For some reason I don't know to this day, I got up and dragged myself along after him. He kept on going. I kept on following. I don't know how far, or why, or on what account. I just did.

"I woke up in a white man's bed. He had my leg cleaned out and put in a splint. When I asked him where I was and how I'd got there, he told me. And that was the funniest part of it. He was a Hudson's Bay Company trapper, just come into the back country the past week to put out his winter line of traps. Right at dusk the day before I came around, he'd heard a wolf howling spit close behind his shack. He'd come out to wing a shot at him and then spotted me, laying in the new snow at the edge of the clearing.

"I stayed with him till I could travel on the leg. It took all winter to mend. In that whole time we had only one visitor, a Red Coat sergeant coming through on his early winter swing to check the district before the big freeze set in. Right after he'd gone, the cold came and we were snowed in till the spring thaw.

"He was a good white man, that old trapper. I even took a part of my name from him, to remember him by. He said it Murray. But the way it came out when I tried it was Murrah. So we just let it stay that way. It pleased him and me both. The Starr part I took from my mother. The Oglala called her Star of the North. I added another r to make it look like a white man's name when I set it down on paper."

The third and final pause was the longest.

"There's not much more, miss," he said at last. "Murray was killed by a trap-line poacher, just before the spring breakup. When I found his body, I knew where I had to go, and how. It was far away from there, and very fast. When the Red Coats came and found me in his cabin, with him and his winter's catch missing, there wouldn't be any questions wasted. Not with a half-breed, and not with that sergeant having seen me staying there with him.

147

"The Mounties were good men. Always fair and easy with the Sioux. But they were still white men. I made a crutch and got out of there. And I was right, miss. This past year I heard about it from a Canuck on his way down to Nome from the Klondike. They're still looking for me back there, miss, and a Canadian murder warrant is surer death than any legal paper Marshal LaMont will ever serve.

"When I left that cabin and headed west, Smoke was waiting for me. God knows how he wintered through, or why he hung around. But there he was before I'd gone a mile, dogging along after me, tail wagging and lonesome whining and lip curling that wolf grin of his, for all he was worth. You can see he's still with me, miss, and maybe now you know why.

"Maybe, too," he finished quietly, "you know, or can guess, why I've told you all this."

She got up, coming slowly around the table to stand just behind him, her voice thick with the tears that trembled behind it.

"Why, Starr?" she whispered wonderingly.

He came around from the stove, facing her but still not looking up. Head hung, thin hands clenched at his sides, he told her the humble rest of it.

"It's that I feel the same way about you, that Smoke feels about me. I'll always follow behind you, girl. Even if it's far back from the trail, only touching you with my eyes, only talking to you with my heart."

"Starr! Oh, Starr . . . !"

Jaw-set gaze still held deliberately downcast, he saw her move instinctively toward him with the low throatiness of the heartfelt cry. Of a sudden, his untamed blood was hammering crazily within him. He flung up his lean head, slant eyes narrowing savagely in response to the apparent invitation in her unguarded gesture. As he did, Erin's face went white with belated fear.

Jaw-set gaze still held deliberately downcast, he saw her move instinctively toward him with the low throatiness of the heartfelt cry. Of a sudden, his untamed blood was hammering crazily within him. He flung up his lean head, slant eyes narrowing savagely in response to the apparent invitation in her unguarded gesture. As he did, Erin's face went white with belated fear.

XI

Too late, the startled settlement girl read the dark warning in the half-breed's wild glance. Too late, she realized that the swart Sioux had sensed her instant of emotional nakedness. Erin O'Farrell had never had a man. But she was a full woman, and no fool.

There came, she knew, a last, still moment between any man and woman, where the artificial barriers of a mutual tongue or common blood melted into nothingness, a lethal, disastrous, point-of-no-return moment where the meaning of a parted lip, a suspended breath, a swift exchange of searching, soul-deep looks flooded uncontrollably past all the arbitrary boundaries of race and reason.

She knew, too, in the frightening half breath of that tiny stillness before Starr came for her, that she had unthinkingly led him far beyond that final division point of civilization and savagery. And she knew, lastly, that to defend herself now was to make a travesty of her entire history with Starr, and a base black lie of every thoughtless look, word, smile, or soft promise with which she had wrongly lured him on to this instant of primitive transgression.

But the time was too far gone for good-girl recriminations. Starr was reaching for her now. There was no mercy in the noiseless half snarl of his Indian-wide mouth, and only unchained ages of brute hunger in the blazing wells of his slitted eyes. Erin knew blind panic, then. She had forced this instant of fearful decision upon herself, and there was no human way in the pitiless Northern world she could avoid its inevitable consequence. In his pagan-proud way, Starr would never understand nor accept a rebuff. Not from a white woman. No matter what she said, or tried to say subsequently, he would feel that his Sioux blood had been the reason for the rejection.

Her hopeless choice, in the fraction of time it took his taloned hands to reach and seize her, was as simple as it was deadly. Either she fought back and lost him, or she surrendered and lost herself.

He had her, then, and there was no more time for thinking. He was like a wild thing, not knowing what he did to her but only that he must do it, and she was more savage than he — whimpering and crying and cursing and tearing at him in helpless defense. His sinewed fingers knotted themselves into the flimsy pinnings of her blanket, ripping the frayed cover from her in a single, growling sweep. As it came away, he hesitated a last, fateful second, held motionless by the pulse-smothering sight of her standing there before him, the hard thrust of her breasts and the satin curve of her soft belly moving wickedly beneath the fire-lit transparency of the clinging nightgown.

It was in that instant that she struck at him with her only remaining weapon. It was an unconscious, cruel thing to do, but there was no conscious thought left in her now. She had made her decision to fight and was doing so on pure instinct, the angry blood of the Celtic forebears running as wildly within her as the dark Sioux strain within Starr.

"Half-breed . . . !" was all she said.

Yet the vicious lash of the word cut into Murrah Starr like a dog whip. For a terrible, soundless instant, his dark face writhed as to the actual slash of the whalebone and sealskin thong. Then, as swiftly and without sound, it went deadly blank. He eased back away from her. Dropping his clenched fists to his sides, he returned his expressionless stare to the rough boards of the cabin floor. It was precisely as if he had not moved from his original, head-hung position, as if the whole ugly moment had never been.

Her voice breaking to the tearful sob that wracked it, and far, far too late, Erin moved pleadingly toward him. "Oh, Starr! Starr! How could you make me do that to you . . . ?"

He shook his head, brought his frozen gaze back up from the floor, stopped her in mid-cry with the Arctic chill of his blue eyes.

"Wonunicun, Wasicun," he muttered thickly in Sioux. *"Woywonihan."* Then, translating in his hesitant, stilted English, and as though with deliberate, soft-slurred cruelty: "I am sorry, white woman. I truly respect you."

"Oh, Starr, you can't, you can't!" she murmured desperately. "I know what you're thinking. I know what you will do. I didn't mean it, Starr. Not the way you took it. Not the way you think. . . ."

"I only think one way, miss" — he was still deliberately slurring his words — "like a half-breed."

When he said that, when he looked at her the way he did when he had said it, she knew she had lost him. And more. That the

153

magic hour and minute of their strange meeting along life's lonely way was forever gone. He would never forgive her. Not any more than she would ever forget him.

"Starr."

"Yes, miss."

"Will you go now?"

He searched her drawn face a long minute, then, surprisingly, shook his head.

"No, I've got to rest. I will stay a little while yet."

"Will you take my bed, then? Please?"

"No. An Indian sleeps on the ground. Like a dog. Where the fire is and where it's warm."

"Starr, please. . . ."

He only looked at her again, his eyes as empty as the winter skies. "I will take this blanket and lie by the stove a little." He bent and picked up the faded cover that, but a moment before, he had torn so ruthlessly from her. "You get back to your bed, miss. I think we are both very tired."

"Starr . . . ?"

"Yes."

"If I do, will you wake me when you go?"

"Why, miss?"

"There is something I have to tell you, and you won't listen now."

"All right, miss. If you want."

154

"I want, Starr," she told him softly. "Very much." She sent the plea to him on the head-bowed wings of a half-sweet, half-sad smile that would have melted the heart of the polar ice pack. But Murrah Starr did not see it.

"Good night, miss," was his only reply. And, with it, he lay down by the dying light of the stove, rolled himself into the blanket, and was still.

XII

In the muffled silence of the cabin Murrah Starr lay restlessly awake. Across the room the old mantel clock stirred reluctantly, chiming the half hour. *Two-thirty,* he thought, and knew that he was not staring into the darkness of Erin O'Farrell's shack but down the sightless distance of the loneliest trail he had ever set out upon. He knew he was going, that he had to go, and why he had to go. There could never be another woman after this one. Not for Murrah Starr. He was like a wolf, he thought. Faithful to his first mate. Seeking out his single female, knowing her when he found her. Staying with her and her alone from that moment until gray age and the long sleep came for both of them.

Once in a rare lifetime, maybe, would a man find a woman like that silken-bodied white girl sighing so gently in her sleep, over there across the cabin blackness. Yet, for

Murrah Starr, to find her was to lose her. That was as sure as an Oglala squaw could tell you the time by the stars. Were he a white man, it might be different. Then he would have ahead of him a whole lifetime with this wondrous woman — a lifetime of lying quietly beside her through the long winters, of feeling the warm skin of that slender body making yours strong again when you were weary or afraid, of smelling the perfumed fragrance of her close to hand in the sunless nights, of seeing the clean, fresh beauty of her by the breakfast fires when spring came and the bright summer lay everywhere in the Northland, and of knowing, day by day, season through season, that she was your mate, that you were hers, and that was the way it would be for as long as you both should draw breath.

But Murrah Starr was not a white man. He was a half-breed. And Erin O'Farrell had reminded him of it in a way and time that could have but one meaning for him. They might meet and make talk and think all sorts of strange and exciting thoughts. But under the bar sinister of his mixed blood, they could never mate.

He knew, being as exquisitely sensitive as any wilderness creature, that she was sorry for what she had said. And that she meant to tell him so before he left. That had been why she had made him promise to awaken her. He sensed, as well, from her standpoint the truth of her claim that she had not meant the whiplash of the hated word to cut him to the heart, but only to drive him back and hold him off until his unwanted passion could cool. But there was the difference of two civilizations between them. Like all Indians, Starr thought and acted in a straight line. Erin had meant what she said at the moment. No later words could ever retract the merciless truth spoken in that unguarded instant.

With the heavy thought, Starr turned for a final, long look toward the dimly visible bunk. The girl was asleep in a dreamless, quiet sleep. She had slept almost at once, as a woman will when she has asked and been given the promise of a second chance. Her breathing now was as peaceful as a child's, her soft body as relaxed as a puppy's. She did not hear the half-breed's muscular form ease free of the tattered blanket and come, cat-easy, to its moccasined feet beside the guttering stove.

Starr moved swiftly then. Within minutes he was ready, had filled the pack, fastened his parka lacings, let the wolf dog out, picked up his Winchester and the snowshoes. In the last moment, his hand already on the door latch, he hesitated.

In his sleepless decision to leave without fulfilling his promise to awaken the girl, he had thought only of himself. Now, suddenly, he was thinking of her. Would it not, after all, be safer to awaken her as she had asked? Let her say what she had to say and then go anyway? Starr knew little of women, red or white. But, like Erin, his lack of experience did not make him simple.

In the unashamed honesty of his savage heart, the unalterable truth of his feelings for her lay like a rock. And like a second rock, as imperishable as the first, lay the certain knowledge that, cruel outburst or no, the white girl returned those feelings without reservation. She had told him that much with every sidelong glance, soft word, or bright, quick smile, since the moment of his returning consciousness in the blessed fragrance of her tiny bunk, following his nearly fatal beating by McClennon and his men.

Now, thinking of that fact, was there not a greater danger of prolonging her share of those impossible feelings by leaving without making finally clear to her the dead certainty that they would never meet again? He thought, desperately, of leaving a note, telling her why he was going away. Why they could never share the same trail. Why he must go his dangerous way and she her decent one. Why his hunted life must never become hers.

But that was what he wanted to tell her, what his heart cried out to say to her — not what he knew he had to make her think. No, he was doing the right thing. She must awaken with the thought that he had tried to take what he wanted of her, and that was all he wanted of her. And, failing in that pure brute attempt, he had slunk away like the half-breed animal they called him in the camps. Any other way, any half-hopeful note left behind, any clumsy awakening farewell made on last-minute weakening impulse could only lead her loyally along after him into the trap McClennon was even now racing to set for him at the Blind Cañon Mine.

Again and finally, no. This other, hard, half-breed way — this deliberate, surly, dumb-brute disappearance — was the only way that would leave her thinking what Starr wanted her to think. It would work with her, he was certain. She was that kind of a woman. Soft with city ways and settlement notions of how decent men should behave. Full of good-girl ideas. Believing in the law and in God and all the other soft lies the white man told himself. Not seeing the evil in men like Angus McClennon, and not wanting to see it. Easy to lead on and to fool. Just as easy to turn on you and to hurt and drive away.

Starr did not take his hand from the latch. For her sake, he had to do this thing now, he told himself. Had to hurt her, as she had hurt him. And she would be hurt, very badly hurt, when she awoke to find him gone. Gone with no good byes, no left-behind excuses, no least heed to the promise he had made her. As surely as the big snows were coming, this careful treachery would make her heart bad for him. Make her hate him and despise him. And, in the bitter years to come, make her finally and forever forget him. That was the way it must always end between a half-breed and a white woman.

Still, in that last instant, Murrah Starr came away from the door. Came to stand in the darkness by the bunk side. To take her slim hand, like he had in the Dry Gulch cave, and to put his wide lips to its cool palm and to hold it thus a long, quiet time against his dark-skinned cheek. He was gone then, leaving it that way, his only good bye the one shy kiss.

He did not look back again. Moments

later, only the peaceful breathing of Erin O'Farrell disturbed the deepening stillness of the weathered shanty in Fishhead Alley.

XIII

Out on the trail, past the town's thick air and lost in the dry, clean world of the outer tundra snows, Starr felt better. The girl was out of the way. It would be just him and wolf now, against McClennon and his nine hired men. Tall odds, but Starr thought they would find him a tall Oglala, hard to trail and hard to take, with Smoke to warn him and the Winchester to back up the wolf dog's alerting whine.

He did not hope to beat them, only to make them know how tough the Sioux half of him would be to kill, and how many of them were going to die finding that out. The latter thought was no idle Indian boast. Toward its deadly end he had made elaborate preparation. It was the thought of that preparation which now lifted the corners of his dark lips and lengthened the sibilant *hush-hush* of his snowshoed stride along the Anvil Creek trail.

It was not a pleasant thought, but Starr was not dealing with pleasant men. The crook of the mirthless grin only twisted wider, the soft slapping fall of the snowshoes grew only more bent-kneed and grimly swift.

It was high noon of that same morning when he came in from the north over the low pass from the Kotzebue River country, to look down upon the south-sprawling valley of the Pushtash Creek drainage. 400 yards below him lay the snow-crowned board and canvas mushrooms of his shack, supply shed, and tiny powder bunker. The snow had slacked off, and, glittering blindingly through a wind-kicked hole in the storm's leaden cloud bank, the sun was washing the whole wild tumble of the Pushtash foothills with its diamond brightness. It was so clear, Starr thought, that a Sioux-trained eye could spot a wood rat dropping on the white breast of that snow down there. But that snow was virgin clean. There was not a single cross-webbed snowshoe track, or the least feathery trace of a sled runner within daylight sight of the Blind Cañon diggings.

Wonderful! He had beaten them there. Old Wakan Tanka was with his Oglala half-son so far. Now, how long would he stay with him? Long enough? Who could say? A man could only wait and pray, and hope that they would come before the darkness so that he could know how they meant to make their camp. Which of them would sleep in the shack itself? How carelessly, or carefully, would they stake out their sled dogs? Above all, where and in what manner would that cursed Chinik Indian bed down?

Past its brief, back-warming meridian the sun dropped with a rush. The temperature plunged with it. The shifting wind knifed through the motionless watcher in the pass, cutting him with its dropping cold, slashing at him with its ground dance of blowing ice slivers. Starr only edged closer to the furry heat of the wolf dog, crouched side-by-side with him on the narrow granite parapet.

A fire for tea or body warmth was out of the question. All he could do was draw outside heat from the windbreak of Smoke's faithful flank and inside warmth from his own deep animal vitality. For to move more than enough to flex a freezing hand or un-cramp an aching set of numbing toes was to invite sharp-eyed disaster.

The Chinik could see as well as Starr could. Better, maybe. Should he happen to be scouting in advance of the other sleds, he might see Starr before Starr saw him, if he made any stand-up stir or disturbance bigger than the frosty vapor of his breath, no matter that he was a quarter mile away and camouflaged by gray granite. The eye-jarring qualities of the least foreign movement in a land so deathly still was beyond belief. But Murrah Starr knew this lethal quiet and he obeyed and became literally a living part of it through the long hours of waiting, wind-cut coldness.

At a quarter of four, with the light going fast and a thin flurry of snow beginning to silver down as the wind dropped, the wolf dog whined and shot his scarred ears down the valley. A moment later Starr heard the sound — the faint jingling of the tiny silver harness bells the Chinik and Selawik tribes used on their lead dogs' breast bands.

It ceased almost as soon as it began, the unearthly hush of the Northland settling once more over the barren amphitheatre below. But he knew what to watch for now, and shortly he saw it — the tall, buck-skinned figure of Tonga Nahahki, gliding through the spruce timber below the Blind Cañon's frozen sluiceway.

The Chinik read the clean snow around the mine buildings as swiftly as had Starr before him. He bore straight in toward the cabin, circled past it, around the outer perimeters of the supply shed and powder bunker, his snowshoes slapping with the same muted speed as the half-breed's. Satisfied that the fresh blanket over the old crust was unbroken from any quarter, he shot the bolt on his Civil War Spencer and fired once into the air downstream over the spruce stands. When the answering, lighter bark of a Winchester echoed upward from the hidden creek trail, he wheeled and shuffled back into the timber the same way he had come.

Starr clearly heard the following crack of his dog whip and the ill-tempered growl of his Chinik — "Go ahead!" — to his lead animal. Seconds later, the straining Kotzebue Huskies broke around the far bend of the ice-clad creek, geed sharply, swung in toward the silent shack. As they did, the half-breed caught the sudden, excited yapping of the other teams.

Good! Everything was working out right, down there. McClennon and the rest were closely behind the Chinik devil. They would be up to the diggings with still a little late twilight to spare.

They came just before the increasing snow and fading light closed off the view from Starr's rocky spire. He saw them stake their dogs in the open-faced shelter of the shed, and grunted another deep Oglala pleasure word. Then he watched all of them except the Indian crowd into the little shack with their blankets and bedrolls. The third Sioux growl of satisfaction cocked Smoke's attentive ears. The Great Spirit was really making up for his past mistreatment of his half-breed stepchild.

But in the last minute Starr was seeing something he had been afraid of from the first, something that was neither good nor pleasurable but very clearly a bad thing, a thing ill-bred and without respect, from the Indian standpoint. The cursed Chinik was refusing the courtesy of his Oglala cousin's house, was bedding down in the open, under the shelter of the shed's south eaves. Worse, he was staking his raw-nerved Kotzebue curs in a careful, full circle around his sleeping spot.

Starr's scowl was darkened by more than the swift shutting off of the Arctic twilight. Well, that saved Tonga Nahahki. At least for tonight. A runt snow bunting could not flit through that ring of trigger-tempered Indian dogs without being spotted and snapped up. A man would simply have to accept that. The pleasant little preamble to his main plan, dedicated to the thoughtful proposition of taking care of McClennon's Chinik bodyguard before getting on with the deadly rest of it, had to be rewritten now.

Perhaps that, too, was as well. The half-breed nodded grimly to himself. He could afford to be philosophical. Knowing what he did, he could afford to be generous. If he could get in past the wary Indian and his half-wild dogs, could get up to that shack full of claim-jumpers, even for sixty precious seconds, Starr would be content to take his following chances with his Chinik brother. For, having entered the lonely little building on the Pushtash, Angus McClennon and his eight half-breed scalp hunters had stepped into a trap as murderous as any ever conceived or set by one man's hand. Should Murrah Starr succeed in springing that trap, Tonga Nahahki would be the only enemy human left alive within forty night-dark miles of the Blind Cañon's frozen diggings.

Wired to the peeled willow underpinnings of that flimsy shack, packed in a greasy-fat yellow bundle with a single thirty-second fuse and lovingly tooth-crimped blasting cap, were eight sticks of DuPont Superior brand dynamite.

XIV

He took Smoke with him, working along the ridge of the low hills inland of the shack. When he came opposite it, he ordered the wolf dog to lie down and wait there. Then he went on down alone.

The snow by this time had cut visibility to fifteen or twenty feet. The wind, dropping with the temperature, still held lightly from the north, putting his course toward the shack safely to the lee of the shed and guaranteeing that the sleeping dogs would not get his scent. Additionally the heavy fall blotted out any chance that the slight sound of his snowshoes would carry to them. His only worry was the Indian bedded south of the shed. He and his nervous Huskies. With the snow coming so heavily, a man had to cut a pretty thin line to make sure he missed them, while still keeping his blind bearing on the shack. But that was part of the gamble. And just the first little part of it.

Starr took it with his Sioux luck on one hand and the blucd steel breech of his Winchester in the other.

In an agonizing ten-minute stalk, putting one snowshoe prayerfully in front of the other and holding up every fourth or fifth step to freeze and listen, he reached the rear of the shack without detection. The next moment he was wriggling in under its familiar foundation stilts, feeling for his dynamite set. He found the stubby fuse and fumbled in his parka for his match case.

Above him he could hear the scrape of booted feet, the low mutter of men talking. They were still awake and moving around. That was not too good. He would rather have waited until they were asleep. But with the weather the way it was — one minute snow squalling point-blank thick, the next clearing off to where a man could see a straightaway mile — he could not risk the delay. He had had to go on in, and fast, while the present flurry was heavy enough to hide him.

He had the match case out now. It was the standard Northland case, an empty .12-gauge shotgun shell telescoped inside a .10 gauge. He pulled it apart with his teeth and his free hand, the other hand not daring to lose contact with the abbreviated fuse. With the first match his good luck began to run roughly. A freak gust of ground snow whirled in under the pilings, putting it out. He tried two more with the same success. And began to sweat a little.

The damned wind was picking up. Those gusts were not freaks. If it continued to rise at this rate, it would blow the little valley clear in a matter of minutes. If it did that, his position under the shack with the stinking Chinik and 200 yards of open ground between him and the hills was the last place in the Pushtash he would want to find himself. Clamping his jaw, Starr tried two more matches. The first one burned down until it seared his fingers, but the frozen fuse would not take. On the second one the warmed coil took, but ran only half an inch. There it sputtered, smoked thinly, died out.

Cursing soundlessly, the half-breed put his sixth match to the section just past the burn out. As its guttering flame got down to his fingers, the fuse spat weakly, faltered, caught again, ran another half inch, fizzled, punked out. In the shotgun shell case, there was one more match.

Starr's helpless fury almost strangled him. In his pack, up there on the ridge with Smoke, he had an oilskin-wrapped factory box of 500. How in the name of anybody's

God had he got himself caught down under that shack with only seven! *Seven?* Seven, hell! He had *one.* One miserable sulphur-dipped sliver of soft pine between him and his last, best chance to hold on to his $1,000,000 mine! In his desperation he hesitated, confused, rattled, undecided about the surest way to try with that final match. As he did, real trouble blew in under the shack on the heels of a suddenly reversing back draft of ground wind.

The gust switched from north to south for thirty full seconds. The abrupt shift drove his perspiring scent squarely into the sensitive nostrils of Tonga Nahahki's Kotzebue Huskies. The Indian dogs burst up out of their covering snow mounds like tundra Ptarmigan, the throaty yammer of their snarls jumping the Chinik out of his blankets, startling the men in the cabin above Starr. He heard the quick alarm of their voices, the hurried scrape of chair legs and the sudden stampeding of boot soles toward the door.

Starr was not afraid. He was furious. Black, ugly, stone-cold furious. In the moment's pause that followed the Huskies' warning uproar, and came ahead of Tonga's silent leap to unchain the first of the wildly baying pack, the half-breed took dead calm

173

stock of his situation. The snow had thinned to nothing in the short minutes he had lain under the shack. The returned wind had done its deadly work behind his back. The north Alaskan night, never truly dark under a clearing sky, even in mid-winter, was growing lighter with every breath he lay there sucking into his tightening chest. Well, all right. If that was the way the gravel washed, a man would pan it the best he could. He still had a handful of seconds before those idiot Chinik curs settled down enough to cut his tracks and run them in under the shack.

He did not hurry, but moved with the deadly precision of a man whose own life no longer meant anything to him, and to whom the lives of those other men still in the shack above him now meant everything. His sheath knife slashed smoothly, severing the already short fuse within inches of its buried detonating cap. The seventh match was scratched, cupped, held to the freshly cut core of the black stub as steadily as though the holder was lighting a good cigar. But in the same instant that the new cut took and started to run hissingly, the first of Tonga Nahahki's dogs was driving in under the shack after Murrah Starr.

He lay on his belly, cheeking the Winchester carefully, not wasting a shot. There were three of the Huskies now, all of them so close he could feel the heat of their slobbering breaths. The first two dropped like they had run into a wall, smashed dead and knocked backward by the face-close burst of the big .44 slugs. The third screamed crazily, channeled from forechest to tail root by the third slug. He thrashed out from under the shack, tripping up McClennon as the latter ran out the door.

The big Scot landed hard, facing the shack. He shook his head clear in time to see under it and catch Starr's silhouette break away from the far side and race for the foothills. In the same instant he saw the half-breed, his eye corner caught the spark and sputter of the burning fuse. His warning roar rose above the compounded clamor of the dogs in the supply shed, now all awake and raging at the ends of their chains.

"God Almighty, lads, get away! Get away! The 'breed's got the shack dynamited!"

Starr was perhaps 150 feet from the shack when it blew. The sledge-hammer blast of the concussion knocked him face forward into the snow, blinding him, deafening him, smashing the side of his head into a snow-covered boulder. He stumbled up, still running, staggering, fighting toward the foothills, the blood from his broken nose and torn scalp filling his eyes with red darkness.

Behind him Tonga Nahahki, swinging across from the shed to cut him off, was tumbled thirty feet and slammed up against a gravel bank, unconscious. His remaining dogs were blown out from around him like furry puffballs. Some were thrown into the air, some driven into the snow, still others blasted spinningly away across the top crust. None of the stunned animals lost his life; all of them lost their interest in running down fleeing half-breeds.

Back at the shack, McClennon's men were not so lucky, yet still far luckier than Murrah Starr had meant them to be. Of the eight, the Faro Kid and five others got far enough out and away to suffer no more than having half a dozen eardrums ruptured and their flying faces driven into the frozen creek gravel, when the tremendous edge of compressed air smashed them between the shoulder blades. Of the other, laggard two, one never got out of the cabin and was subsequently identified only by bits and pieces, the largest whole specimen of which was the attached hand, wrist, radius, and elbow of a left arm. The second man was ten strides beyond the door when Starr's fifteen-second fuse ran out. He was hurled forty feet across the creek, impaled on a cross-brace timber projecting from the half-breed's sluice-box flume. He was still alive when they pulled him free of the pinning spar.

When a dozen shallow breaths later, the hole in the wounded man's chest quit pumping blood, Murrah Starr's dark score stood graven, Indian deep, in the numbed minds of the seven white survivors. And beneath its grim total was etched the uneasy script of a frighteningly simple question. He had killed five men in nine days. How long would it take him to kill seven more?

XV

That night it began to get cold — really
cold. Starr kept a spare thermometer hung
on the inside south wall of the supply shed.
When McClennon had gathered his remaining posse members in that shelter, the
mercury was standing at five above. It had
dropped fifteen degrees in the half hour
since the explosion. By 2:00 a.m. it was
down to twelve below. When the hoarfrost
of first daylight crept over the Pushtash
foothills long hours later, the thin red line
was out of sight past the last mark on the
glass's chipped scale — minus twenty-five.

"Thirty-five below, be-Jesus," guessed Big
Tim Rafferty, huddling with McClennon
and the Faro Kid over the stirred-up fire,
waiting for the tea water to boil. "Sure and
it's the divil's own beauty of a drop for but
the second week in October."

"Thirty-five, mon. Maybe forty," amended
McClennon thoughtfully. Both his compan-

ions glanced up quickly at the patent burr of pleasure in his heavy voice.

Given ten hours in the fire-warmed shelter of the shed to recover from the nasty surprise of Starr's dynamite plant, the dour Scot's mind was back on bull-headed schedule. Angus McClennon was that rare accident of inheritance — the man born without the feeling of fear or the knowledge of failure in him. He simply did not understand what it meant to be afraid of any living thing. From boyhood his tremendous physique had made him easy, bullying master over his environment. And that environment had been composed of a society of men as tough and as quirky and dangerous as any in frontier history. This sheer physical superiority, coupled with a wolf-quick intellect and the uncertain temper of a trapped grizzly, did not add up to a total that could be long intimidated — not even by eight sticks of dynamite.

"Either way, lads," he now concluded, brow knit, "it's certain bad news for half-breeds, this cold snap setting in back of this new snow."

Big Tim wagged his shaggy head, palmed his ham-sized hands.

"Faith now, McClennon, and I kin never follow yez when ye're talkin' about this mur-

179

derin' whelp, Starr. He downs three of us last week with his darlin' rifle and yez tell us he's fixed himself fer sure. Now it's two more of our lads by way of more blastin' powder than them Cuban monkeys lit off under Admiral Dewey. And when, on top of that, the blessed mercury dives so far down in the bulb yez can't see it with a spyglass, ye take sober oath it's sad tidin's and the sound of harps fer half-Injuns. Yez lost me the first dance, laddie buck. Would yez mind waltzin' me around once more?"

McClennon looked at him. "Ye talk too much, Rafferty. Hold yer Irish tongue."

Big Tim knew his man. When Black Angus got quiet and short like that, it was high time a wise lad took heed. Timothy Francis Xavier Rafferty had not gotten to be the number two man in the Miner's Association by blarney alone. He surrendered the floor.

McClennon acknowledged the courtesy with a slow nod, plodded methodically ahead with his interrupted weather forecast and what it meant in terms of trapping half-breeds. The present freeze, he estimated, would last the rest of the week. With clear weather the fleeing half-breed could not chance more than a five-minute fire to boil tea. What food he had was in the pack on his back. When that was gone, he was all through. No game would be stirring in such a sub-zero snap. Even if it were, the fugitive would scarcely dare risk the locating sound of a rifle shot.

Now, then. Where it was true the hard old crust just under the new fall made for good snowshoeing, it made for even better dog sledding. Far worse than that for the doomed half-breed, such a six-inch fresh topping as yesterday's flurry put on, made for perfect tracking. They still had two full malamute sled teams, could use Tonga's surviving dogs for trailers. The supply shed, built snugly against the gravel bank that had saved it when the shack went up, would make an even better base camp than Starr's miserable hut. It was bigger and better built, could be easily closed in on its open side with lumber from the demolished shack. They had supplies for at least a month and no reason whatever to push their return to Nome. Nothing was going to happen back there during their absence.

This sharp freeze would build up the shore-ice rapidly. Before week's end, in all probability, the last ship out for the States would clear the roadstead and be gone. There was always the outside chance that some daft skipper would put in during the little time remaining. But that was about as much of a gamble as betting four aces, buried, against a pair of treys showing. No, the half-breed was done. He did not have a chance.

What could he do? Where could he possibly go? And, wherever he might try to go, on foot as he was, how long could he hope to stay ahead of two crack dog teams and the best Indian tracker north of Seward Peninsula? "No, by God!" the glowering owner of the mercantile repeated triumphantly. With Nome sealed off by LaMont's murder warrant and the other settlements, from Golovin Bay up to the Kawalik Lagoon, alerted against him, the half-breed was trapped. All they had to do was stay on his trail until they ran it into the last spruce thicket. And that was that.

In the final hand for the $1,000,000 pot of his Blind Cañon bonanza, Murrah Starr was holding a bobtailed flush; he had one week's food, a rifle, a pair of snowshoes, a tame wolf. That was a four-card hand any way you wanted to count it. How could he possibly draw out on them?

In answer to the belligerent challenge of the closing question the Faro Kid, who had not opened his thin mouth so far, spat into the fire, unburdened himself.

"You're forgettin' one thing," he drawled

softly. "A full hand deals five cards where I come from."

McClennon lost his aggressive, blunt-jawed grin, scowled blackly.

"Say what ye mean, mon."

The lean gunman shrugged. "In my game, the 'breed's holdin' a bad kicker, that's all."

"Aye? Such as what, now, lad?"

"Such as more cold guts than you could stuff in a six-hundred-pound steer with a snow shovel," said the Faro Kid.

When Erin awoke, the late daylight was graying the interior of the little shack in Fishhead Alley. She yawned lazily, stretched like a young lioness luxuriating in the pleasant drowsiness following a long nap in summer sunlight. Her slender arms lay outflung for a lingering moment, then closed with the slow, semiconscious smile of expectant reward — on nothing.

She was fully awake then, her sudden alarm and the growing daylight widening her green-blue eyes. The cabin was empty. Starr and the wolf dog were gone.

She dressed quickly, opened the stove draft, boiled coffee, sat down at the rickety table to begin the bad process of thinking back — and the worse one of thinking ahead. There was no nonsense of "morning after" shame in the Irish girl. No more than there had been in Murrah Starr before her. She recognized what had happened, as had he, for what it honestly was: an instinctive accident of time and place. A thing that neither of them had sought, for which neither of them was responsible, and the consequences of which both would have to face and figure out.

It was at this point, however, that the thinking of Erin O'Farrell and Murrah Starr diverged as abruptly as a north-south trail fork. It was clear to her, and becoming more clear as the hot black coffee got into her, that she was not going to see the half-breed again. Not if he had his lone-wolf way about it. There was simply that empty feeling of inevitability about the whole thing — the way he had shown up shadowing his would-be killers through the night, the way he had read her mind when she had started to tell him she could not help him any more, the way he had asked her to wait and not to say it, and had then told her his strange story.

The settlement girl grimaced at the memory and the unhappy hindsight it now brought her. That story had been Starr's way of saying good bye. He had known that, every soft word of its telling. Had he not, he would never have uncovered his savage heart the way he did at the ending. As he had stood there telling it to her, even in the last minute of his poignantly poetic Indian way of saying "I love you," he had known they would not meet again. What had followed had been her doing, not his. He had come only to say good bye. Now he had said it and was gone.

He meant never to come back. His way of going told a girl that. And more. It told her that he had meant it to hurt her. To disillusion her. To break the trail between them forever. But it was precisely there, that Murrah Starr had been wrong about Erin O'Farrell.

The sensitive Irish girl understood him better than he understood himself. His dead-of-the-night desertion of her had been anything but the natural brutality of an ignorant, lustful half-breed, which he had assumed she would think it was. It had, instead, been the unselfish act of an uncivilized, strangely gentle savage who had loved her enough to leave her in the only moment of real happiness he had ever found, or could ever hope to find again.

It was a deeply flushed, disturbingly excited Erin O'Farrell who, minutes later, stood fastening the neck laces of her parka

185

in the open door of the shack, and who gazed up Fishhead Alley, out across the empty stillness of the tundra, toward the distant Pushtash. The low-voiced vow was made half aloud and haltingly soft to the lonely whistle of the tundra wind, just before she turned swiftly for Front Street and the office of U.S. Marshal Harry La-Mont.

"Last night you asked me if I still wanted to help you. You didn't wait for your answer then. Can you hear it now? It's yes, Starr. God forgive me, it always was and always will be . . . !"

XVI

Starr's first thought was only for putting distance between himself and McClennon's badly shaken posse. He had to get far enough away to make a little fire, eat, and rest. He had not slept in forty-eight hours, nor had any warm food in twenty-four. As he went now, stumbling toward the rocky hills, his head was still ringing from the blast. His legs felt strangely weak and his belly like everything inside him had been torn loose and pushed down into his loins. By the time he had climbed the ridge and groped along it for 200 or 300 feet, he knew something else, something that somehow filled him with a sudden, nameless dread, and yet which was not possible, which could not be possible.

He was lost. Not a quarter mile from his Blind Cañon strike, on a ridge whose every pebble he knew as well as he knew his face in the cracked shaving mirror above his shack's wash basin, Murrah Starr was lost. In some impossible way he had missed the plain line of his own tracks, had not topped out where he should have. Neither was the faithful Smoke where he had left him. Or was he? The chill of the thought brought him to a halt. In four long years, the wolf dog had never disobeyed him. But that was crazy. He must have moved. Starr shook off the wild doubt, stumbled on.

But the early night, blown free and clear as he knew it must now be from the continuing whip of the wind, was far too dark. When, for the third time in as many minutes, he tripped over an unseen granite outcropping and fell heavily, he did not get up. He lay there, the sickening truth draining his little remaining strength.

There was nothing wrong with the wind and its biting work. The night was clear. No rock had shifted from its familiar position on the ridge top since he had gone down off of it a half hour before. Smoke had not moved an obedient muscle from the spot where he had downed him. No, there was nothing wrong with the weather or the rocks or the wolf dog. But there was something very wrong with Murrah Starr — bad, wicked, belly-queasing wrong. He was blind. He was blind as a weanling cave bat, sightless as a week-old wolf whelp, helpless as a hamstrung caribou calf. He was down and dead and all done as a swallowed mouse in a horned owl's belly.

The pure panic of it set him wild at first. He dug at his eyes, scooped up fresh snow and scrubbed them out, beat at them crazily with the heels of his knotted fists. Nothing happened. Not a glimmer broke through. Not a shadow or a shape or a sound of movement showed anywhere about him. It was true! He could not see!

But the terrible realization acted as its own sedative. His racing mind slowed, reason returned, he began to think. He had seen both men and animals in shock before. He remembered from far back in his boyhood how it had happened with Little Hawk, his first dog, a Slave Lake Indian puppy given him by old Tatanka on his eighth birthday. An angry old black bear sow they were trailing had turned on Little Hawk and slapped him head over heels. The puppy had blundered around camp, bumping into things for a week, before he got his sight and senses back. Then there was that other time when Lame Horse, the Oglala's best hunter, had been lost in a blizzard for five days without food or fire and they had found him walking in empty circles not 500 yards from the teepees, out of his head and stone blind for three days following, before rest and good care had repaired his shattered nerves and let him see again.

But where such desperately dug-up memories of blinding shock and subsequently restored sight might quiet a man's panic long enough to let him start thinking that he himself might see again, they as quickly plunged him right back into the bottom of the pit. Three days! A week! Good God. Murrah Starr had eight, maybe ten hours! And that long, only at best. Only if the blast had hurt McClennon and his men as badly as it had Starr, badly enough to hold them up until daylight brought back their courage and made the half-breed's wobbling trail up the ridge plain enough for a settlement boy to follow. That was all he could hope for. Starr knew that.

Looking back over his shoulder as he had run for his own life, just before the shack went up, he had seen enough to let him know his dynamite trap had sprung shut seconds too late. He had seen the Chinik cutting across from the shed, only short yards behind him, had seen, past him and fleetingly, the shadows of at least four or five men getting safely clear of the doomed shack. And he had seen, in the sweating instant of wriggling clear of the shack's underpinnings, McClennon himself fall and crash flatly on his thick belly not ten feet from him. He knew, as well, that the huge Scot had gotten up and cleanly away — more, that he had seen Starr and noted the ridge top direction and intent of his flight.

No, there was no hope that they were hurt badly enough to abandon his trail for more than the rest of the night. He had those short hours until first light between him and them, maybe. Then they would be up here after him, coming up to find him lying there in those rocks, staring at them empty-eyed. Not seeing but only hearing the loading clank of the Winchester action that would come just ahead of the smash of the blunt .44 slug into his blind face.

Starr sank forward into the snow. He lay still for many minutes. Then, with the blowing snow beginning to mound and build up along his body, he heard something, or thought he did. He stirred, raised his head. He could see now! My God, he could see! It was a wolf, a young wolf caught in a trap and dragging a heavy chain and trap log behind him through the snow. It was standing over there in the darkness at the edge of the trees, staring at him and whining and wagging his tail.

Starr shut his eyes. There were no trees on that ridge. How could there be a wolf standing at their edge? When he opened his eyes again, the wolf was gone and he knew that his mind was growing sick. But was it? He had thought the same thing that other time so long ago in the deserted Oglala village. Yet the wolf had really been there. It had come in to him and laid down closely beside him when he spoke and called out to it. And it had gotten him up, taken him on, led him safely away from there. Led him?

Was that the thought that stayed in his mind now? That fought and demanded to be felt? To be answered? God damn you, Smoke, where are you? Wolf friend, cousin, are you there again? Do you hear me now? Come closer, come closer. I can't see you. . . .

The half-breed broke off the hoarse jumble of Sioux gutturals, and pursed his bruised lips. The whistle that had made Erin shiver the night in the Dry Gulch Cañon cave quavered plaintively. It was picked up by the vagrant wind, whirled off down the ridge top, buffeted carelessly away and wasted against the unlistening granite ledges. This time, when Starr went forward into the snow, he did not raise his head again.

■ ■ ■ ■

He did not know how much time had passed. He only felt the dig and urgent drive of the rough, long-nailed pads against his side and the bunt and shove of the broad muzzle nosing under his slack head. He did not like it and struck out heavily, ordering the wolf dog in thick angry Sioux to go away and leave him alone. Then the hot wet scrape of the whimpering animal's tongue, sharp and painful as a wood rasp, was raking the raw flesh of his face, and Murrah Starr came suddenly, joltingly back to bell-clear consciousness.

Sotaju! Smoke! This was no dream. No creeping mind-sickness. The big ugly devil was actually there! To be touched, smelled, cursed at, reached for, gathered happily in, clung to, and cradled like a four week's puppy!

The strength came back into Starr in heat-prickling waves. The way it did, carrying its stabbing pain clear down into the freezing ends of his hands and feet, let him know he could not have laid there more than bare minutes before the wolf dog scented him out and found him. He must have heard the whistle, been close when he did, followed his wonderful nose upwind without a single false cast through the naked rocks between them. Any other way, any more time taken than that handful of minutes, and Starr knew the sub-zero wind would have frozen him stiff as a slab of January dog salmon.

As it was, he was all right. His head was quiet, his ears clear, his mind sharp. Only his eyes were still gone. But he had Smoke now. He had a wolf's eyes now. And a wolf's strength and guts and bright mind to lean on and hang to and let lead him away.

Yes, they would still get him, those white sons-of-she-dogs down there. Them and their slack-jawed whelp of a Chinik camp cur. But they would not get him just by walking up the ridge and pumping a .44 slug into him or knocking his head in with a rifle butt. They would have to come after him now, by God, blind or not blind!

His fingers fumbled at his parka, unstringing its six-foot breast lace. He made the slender thong fast to the wolf dog's collar ring, wrapped the free end about his right hand, took his Winchester in his left, and growled a savage order in Sioux.

Minutes later the wolf dog had led him to the spot where he had been told to stay beside the precious pack. Starr felt for it, found it, shouldered into it. He called Smoke to him, knotted the buckskin leash once more about his lean fist. "*Wan'howo, Sotaju. Ya'howo!* Let's go, Smoke. Now! Fast! Far away from here!"

The wolf dog whined, looked back and up into the dark, staring face above him. He made a sound deeply in his throat, as near to a dog sound as a wolf can come. Then he started off, leaning into his collar just enough to keep the leash taut, not enough to hurry his master or draw him off balance or stumble him into any least obstruction.

He picked his own way, as quickly and surely of where he set his big splayed pads as a stalking cat. His yellow eyes bored unblinkingly ahead, missing no turn or twisting of the trail that might insure clean footing for the man behind him. In all the long, tortuous way southward down the rugged spine of the ridge above the Pushtash, as far through the Arctic night gray as a narrowed human eye might have followed them, the watchful brute did not falter once, or the blank-eyed half-breed stumble a single time.

XVII

Starr lost all track of time and distance as Smoke led him through the night. He knew they were going south, at first, from the way the ridge fell off where it came to level ground about three miles below the shack. Then, after another long stretch, the odor of spruce and the occasional slap of a trailside branch told him they were into the timber. He guessed, from that, that they were still heading south. But when, sometime later, Smoke veered sharply to the left and began to climb he gave up trying to orient himself. He could only guess, again, that after the instinctive habit of the wolf his silent guide was making for high ground in search of a place to bed down. He was right.

Minutes after turning away from the timbered flats, the wolf dog halted. He whined eagerly, bunted demandingly at Starr's leash hand. The half-breed let him go, so weary now that it took all the effort he could summon just to fumble for the chain collar and untie the parka thong from it. He stood, legs braced, exhausted body swaying, while the wolf dog worked around him in a cautious circle, snuffling and scenting out the bedding spot.

Apparently the place met with the latter's wary approval, for the next moment he had come again to Starr's side. Rearing gently, he placed his splayed forefeet on the half-breed's chest, nuzzled his cheek, growled, dropped back to all fours.

Starr armed out of the pack, let it fall. Sinking to his knees, he was surprised to feel that he was on a bed of packed earth and old spruce needles, entirely free of snow. Shortly he realized that he could no longer feel the wind. At the same time he became aware of a familiar musty odor lingering in the dead air of the place. Wolf smell! Old and stale and baffling at first scent, but unmistakable once recognized. It could mean only one thing. Smoke had brought him to an abandoned whelping den somewhere in the high rocks inland of the creek.

Knowing what he did of such places and the brute cunning with which they were invariably selected, the half-breed realized that once again the big wolf's uncanny intelligence had come between Murrah Starr and certain death. For what little time might remain to him, he would be safer in that rocky, rank-smelling lair than in any other hiding place in the Pushtash. The relief of the thought, along with the wind-sheltered, musty warmth of the granite cavern, were too much for the nerve-worn half-breed. While his fingers were still fumbling with the straps of the pack, to open it and eat before he fainted, he slumped forward and remembered no more.

Smoke came up to him, nosing his still form carefully. Evidently satisfied with the sniffing inspection, he turned around three times and lay down by his side, blunt muzzle pointed toward the opening of the shallow chamber. When, many hours later, the slight change in the outer darkness warned that another short October day was beginning, neither man nor wolf dog had moved. The only sign of life to either of them was the occasional flickering blink of the latter's yellow eyes, as they continued to hold unwaveringly on the den's entrance. It was perhaps half an hour after the first faint stain of daylight appeared that Smoke raised his huge head and began to growl.

The dogs that Tonga Nahahki drove for Mc-

Clennon were all Kotzebue Huskies of the same fierce breed and teammates of the leader Smoke had killed in Nome. Sled dogs were the big Scot's sole hobby. He had taken over a year to make up the team Tonga handled. They were a beautifully matched string of nine originally, now reduced to five by courtesy of the half-breed and his fellow wolf. But those five were enough.

Like most Indian dogs they had been broken to hunt and track as well as back pack and pull a sled or travois. When the Chinik set them on Starr's scent at the edge of the splintered shack, they took off along the wavering line of snowshoe wafflings as whimperingly sure of themselves as so many full-blooded wolves.

At first there was not even any need for their superior noses. They could see the snowshoe tracks as clearly as their sullen master could and, like all the wolf breed, were natural sight hunters in addition to delicate scent trailers. They held up at the spot where Starr had been blown into the snow by the blast, yelping and milling in their eagerness over the blood found there. Tonga came up, read the plain sign of the half-breed's injury from the stiff black hairs adhering to the frozen stain on the boulder against which Starr had struck his head in falling. With a pleased grunt he gave the excited dogs the Chinik go ahead command. To the hoarsely growled — *"Kill-a-muck, kill-a-muck! Hi-eee-yah-hah!"* — they leaped forward in full cry again.

On the ridge, minutes later, they held up for the second time where the unconscious half-breed had laid among the rocks. Here Tonga took longer, for there was more to read and it was not so clear. But once he had scowled out the confusion of the multiple sign and unraveled it as far as the double set of departing snowshoe and wolf tracks leading southward down the ridge, he called the angry dogs off and returned to the shed.

His report to McClennon, who had been arousing and readying his companions meantime, was delivered in such a rich mixture of pure Chinik and bastard trade-English that the other men could not follow it and had to wait for the intently listening Scot to translate it for them. This he did with that bulldog display of his nicotine-rotted teeth that his followers had learned to accept for a grin.

"Tonga says we've got him! All we have to do is go out and pick him up!"

"Six gets you ten," drawled the Faro Kid

laconically, "that he picks some tough."

McClennon broke his grin long enough to answer the lean Westerner with a belligerent jaw thrust, then swept on tensely. "He's hurt. Tonga thinks pretty bad. Either one of the dogs got to him under the shack, or he got hit with something from the blast. There's blood and hair on a rock halfway to the hills, more blood, aye, and a lot more, up on the ridge itself. He was down in both places, stayed down in the second one longer than somewhat. Aye, by God!" he snapped, favoring the blank-faced Chinik with another of his good dog pats on the shoulder, "and he'll stay down in the third one longer yet! *No chock-la-rootin,* Tonga mon?"

"No chock-la-rootin," echoed the Indian expressionlessly.

"Now, then," he went on, "we'll go three ways to make sure we don't miss him. "Sandy, lad, ye and Pierce take one of the sleds and cross over to the ridge to run down the next valley over. Burris, ye and Reed take the other and follow down the creek on this side. Tonga and me will take the loose dogs and run the track on the ridge. Kid, ye and Rafferty stay here and see that he doesn't try doubling back to raise some more hell around here while we're gone. Tonga and me will meet the rest of ye at the foot of the ridge, providing the 'breed hasn't meantime come down off of it some place. If he has, one or the other of ye will cut his track. If ye do, fire three shots and we'll come down. Otherwise, we'll all come together down below and follow out from there in one bunch. Any of ye got anything that's bothering ye, get it out now."

For a few seconds his only answers were the nods of doubtful understanding from the four posse members chosen to man the sleds. Then he caught the Faro Kid's cynical grin.

"All right, mon, what's eating ye? Ye got something to say?"

"Yeah." The still-eyed gunman nodded. "Thanks."

"For what now, lad?"

The Kid's growing acidity about the prospects of an extended season on part-Indian claim owners in the Upper Pushtash was beginning to eat into the glowering Scot's ugly temper. His too-soft query let the other know as much. But the Nevada gambler did not bluff worth two cards to the middle of an inside straight.

"For leavin' me at the shack with Rafferty," he said, his thin smile showing a sudden wrinkle of scum ice around its edges.

"Take my word for it, mister. I ain't lost no wounded half-breeds."

XVIII

In Nome, the color in the coarse gravel of Murrah Starr's chances was thinning out as swiftly as it was in the distant Pushtash. Erin found that out in the first sixty seconds after she had aroused LaMont's two deputies from the dark-mouthed depths of a slumber not made any more pleasant-tasting by some four pints of Seattle rotgut absorbed the night before.

Jack Cushman, the marshal's chief deputy, laid it out for her in four-letter words.

LaMont was still down at Golovin Bay. God alone knew or cared when he would be back. Meanwhile, warrant or no warrant, Cushman and the other deputy, Lew Stillwell, were aiming to sit right squarely on their dead ends until told otherwise by Harry LaMont — in person. They had been out after Starr once already, anyway. And once, after that red-gut so-and-so, was twice too many. Especially with the weather turning off like it was.

Had Miss O'Farrell had a look at a thermometer this morning? Or was that asking too much? The mercury had been out of sight since midnight last night. It was back up around fifteen below right now, but would drop another ten degrees come early afternoon. Did the young lady have any decent idea what that would mean by tonight in the interior? Fifty below. Maybe fifty-five.

Why, even the flat faces over across the river in Eskimo Town were turning their sleds upside down and calling their dogs in. No, ma'am. If two white men could be found between San Francisco and Wrangel Island who would set out upriver in cold like that just to tell Angus McClennon not to be naughty, their names were certainly not Cushman and Stillwell.

If that was not enough, there was more. McClennon was not breaking the law by going out after the half-breed on his own. Far from it. Provided he brought him in alive or dumped him under the ice somewhere upriver, Miner's Association sentiment in Nome would consider him to be doing a public service. Particularly if he left him under the ice. That way it would save the town the cost of the dog salmon and driftwood needed to take him through the winter in the hoosegow.

No, there was just nothing LaMont's men could, or would, do to prevent McClennon from running down the half-breed, if that was what he had in mind. From where they sat, Miss O'Farrell had two shots she could take. If she was half smart, she could go home and wait for LaMont to get back, leaving the question of McClennon's posse up to the marshal, where it rightly belonged. If she wanted to play it stubborn, she could go on down the street to the Association building and put her problem up to Colonel Johnson. Or hadn't she noticed those troopers patrolling Front Street?

Yes, miss, the military was in town. Nome had been under martial law since ten o'clock last night. And anybody should be able to see how simple that made it for the United States Marshal's office. Until the Army pulled out, Deputies Cushman and Stillwell had no more authority in Nome than the young lady herself.

Stunned, still unable to believe that the same two men who had helped her save Starr's life the night of the fight with McClennon would now sit shruggingly by and let him be killed, Erin left LaMont's office and headed for the Association headquarters.

Colonel Pruett Henry Johnson was not a raw-bourbon-and-no-water man like LaMont's deputies. He was in much better shape that morning than they, far more inclined toward sympathy with Miss Erin O'Farrell and her report of justice about to be outraged. He used eight-letter words and a fatherly pat on the shoulder to tell her the same thing they had.

He was in Nome only to maintain law and order in the town itself, and that only until the expected refusal writ arrived from the States — if it did. That *if* could cover any length of time from tomorrow till the 1900 thaw. Meantime, the Army could do no more than to protect the rights of Nome's foreign-born miners in the immediate area of the beach claims. The back country would have to police itself. If Miss O'Farrell's half-breed friend had struck the mother lode forty miles from Nome, that was his problem. There was no way in the Alaskan world that Colonel Johnson could help him. No commander, certainly no West Point man, would dream of attempting to spread 120 troops thin enough to garrison the remote upriver claims. If he could succeed in keeping blood off the beach, Colonel

Johnson would be doing enough to win his brigadier's star.

Seeing the look that crossed his visitor's face, and not impervious to the charms of that face with or without its present withering glance of accusation, the colonel felt for words. If and when the writ from Washington arrived, he assured her vaguely, the situation would be much improved. At that time she could present her problem to the United States Marshal's office with every hope of co-operation. Meanwhile, Colonel Johnson presented his compliments and hoped that were further need to arise while he was still in Nome, the young lady should not hesitate to call upon him again.

Erin turned away angrily. The only thing she thought of doing in connection with Colonel P.H. Johnson required no hesitation. All she wanted at that moment was to get out of his stuffy office as fast as she could.

But where civil and military law had refused to intercede, providence, in the form of a flustered courier, now did so. The excited trooper burst in through the street door, colliding full force with Erin on her way out. The youth was overcome enough by the soft-bodied feel of the brief contact, and by his subsequent honest stare at the

Irish girl's eye-popping good looks, to forget what had brought him sprinting all the way from the beach.

"Uh, beg pardon, miss!" He swept off his ear-flapped fur kepi with a proper flourish and an improper appraisal of the shape that not even a sealskin parka could camouflage. "Reckon I didn't see you, miss. Sorry to have startled you."

Pruett Johnson was a man of considerable sensitivity, tact, control. For a full chicken colonel, he was possessed of an admirable touch of Army humor. He now moved out from behind his desk, inclined his good gray head soberly toward Erin. "Miss O'Farrell, Corporal Bivins. Perhaps I should say the late Corporal Bivins. I don't believe you two have met."

But Bivins was smitten deeply. For the first two seconds it did not sink in. He actually got as far as — "Glad to know you, miss." — before sanity and six years in the regular Army came back on him with a strangling gasp. "Beg pardon, Colonel Johnson, sir!" With his corporal's stripes already as good as ripped off, the stampeded trooper's stance would have shamed a Southern Baptist preacher with the devil's smoking poker shoved up under the tails of his frock coat. "Sergeant Meany just sent me up from the beach, sir. There's a ship from the States just hove to out yonder."

"A ship! What ship, Bivins?"

"A coast guard gunboat, sir. The *Nelly Forsythe*."

"All right. Go on, go on!"

"Well, sir, Colonel Johnson, sir" — the young soldier was excited again, remembering his big news — "a petty officer and a couple of sailors just rowed in. Hit the beach not five minutes ago. Meany, he said to shag on up here on the double and leave you know. They got a U.S. Commissioner from San Francisco aboard, sir. He's got that there miner's order from Washington, D.C. with him. You know the one, sir. About these here bohunkie furriners in Nome. Well, sir, you won't believe it, but the gov'ment done stood up for the dang' square heads right down the line! Ain't that the limit, sir?"

"It's the law, Bivins," corrected Johnson quietly. "And high time. Was there anything else, Corporal?"

Thankful to have his stripes back so easily, Bivins blurted ahead. "Yes, sir. That there petty officer, he told us the commissioner is coming ashore in the captain's gig, right off. He wants a meeting of the miners called this morning, soon's he gets in. Says

210

they got to sail ag'in on tonight's tide. You know, sir, account of the ice forming so fast and all."

"I know, Bivins. All right, get back to the beach. Tell Meany to bring the commissioner up here the minute he lands. Send in the corporal of the guard on your way out. Hop it now!"

When the door banged shut behind the saluting trooper, and before the guard corporal banged it back open, Johnson turned thoughtfully to Erin, still standing by the door trying to make some hopeful sense of the startling news.

"It's not much, miss," said the gray-haired officer gently, "but I'll just suggest it for what it might be worth. If you can manage to locate this McClennon, perhaps you can slow him down with what you've just heard. It will be official in forty-five minutes. The government has ruled against the Miner's Association and they will simply have to accept the situation. I can guarantee you that it will now go very hard with anyone interfering with the foreign-born claim owners. I am quite sure that fact will carry sobering weight with your Mister McClennon. Particularly since he is the Association's president and, I understand, personally responsible for originating the anti-foreign petition." He put his hand to her shoulder. "I honestly wish I could send a squad with you, miss, believe me. But I can't. My authority here expires the minute the commissioner reads that writ of refusal to the Association. Whatever help you can expect now, will have to come from your constituted civil authorities here in Nome. In that regard, you can trust Marshal LaMont completely. He's a fine man and will do what is right."

Yes, thought Erin bitterly. *He was, and he would.* But what in God's sacred name could Marshal LaMont, or any other man, do that would be right for a half-breed Indian after he had been put under two feet of blue river ice by Angus McClennon? Yet, to the solicitous officer, she only bobbed her head, murmured her low thanks, moved quickly for the door, her tired mind grasping desperately at the straw of Johnson's suggestion.

Maybe he was right. Maybe the news from Washington did give her an outside chance of stopping McClennon in time. But even if it did, she still had to figure out some way to get the news to the Blind Cañon Mine. To find somebody who knew where the mine was and who would show her the way there. It was her only chance of saving Starr.

Somehow she had to make it.

But back out in the chill fog of Front Street, her newly stirred excitement slowed and shortly froze solid. Just how did a nineteen-year-old settlement girl go about making the half-breed's one slim chance pay off? Where did she turn now? Who could she ask to help her?

If the Territorial marshal's office would not, and the United States Army could not move to prevent McClennon from committing a cold-blooded murder, who would, or could? The answer was obvious, and hopeless. There was only Erin O'Farrell left to help the lonely half-breed. And who was there left to help her? Nobody. Not a solitary soul. Other than Starr, she had made just one sure friend in Nome — Father Jacquet, the Pribilof *padre.* And what good was a priest at a time like this? Especially one like Nome's variously called "Mad Roosian" and "Teddy Bear"? He could scarcely speak English, conducted all his services in a weird scramble of Russian and Latin, acted as quirky around the little parish house she took care of for him as he did when striding down Front Street with his bearskin coat on in the middle of summer, chanting the *"Ave Maria"* in Ukrainian at the top of his *basso profundo* lungs. Still, the beset girl's mind grounded on the thought of the bearded priest. He was a man of God, for all his eccentricities and outlandish accent. Where else, but to God, could a faithful girl turn now?

White-faced, growing sicker inside with every stumbling step, Erin turned away up Front Street, north, toward the end of town and the Russian *padre*'s tiny church at the edge of the tundra.

Whether it was actually the good Lord working overtime in his last parish north, or simply the ubiquitous shamrock of the Old Sod's luck, Erin never knew. Nor had she time to care. Things happened too fast in those next fifteen minutes.

She found Father Jacquet, grizzly fur parka tucked up around his waist, out in his coal shed helping Arkko Karvinin whelp a first-time malamute bitch. The latter, a squat Finn who had spent his last two summers working one of the best claims on Anvil Creek and the accompanying winters driving dog sled for Nome's peripatetic defender of the faith, was something of a local character in his own close-mouthed right.

His Anvil Creek strike, beyond Starr's fabled find on the Pushtash, was probably the richest in Nome's short, $16-an-ounce history. Yet despite his vast prospective wealth, he chose to divide his time, from first snow fly till the river ice went out in June, piloting Jacquet around the 200-mile swing of his Bering Sea parish.

He was an unfriendly, stolid man who spoke little English and had no close companions in Nome's rigidly anti-foreigner society. Fate had him already set aside for a bloody rôle in the coming year's great battle for the beach at Norton Sound. Now, in the moment of Erin O'Farrell's breathless arrival in the coal shed's door, she put the first touch of that dark future's hand to the shoulder of the brooding Finn. For Arkko Karvinin was no more an American citizen than Murrah Starr. And it had been he who headed the foreign-born claim owners' delegation that had brought Colonel Johnson and martial law marching into Nome the night of McClennon's secret departure for the Blind Cañon Mine.

Indeed, Fortune, had she sat up all winter trying, could not have picked a more bitter witness than Arkko Karvinin to station in Father Jacquet's ramshackle coal shed that long-gone morning of October 9, 1899. It was he, now, and not the Russian priest, who answered the distraught Irish girl when

215

she had gasped out her story.

All that the good father added to his companion's gruff reply to Erin was the sign of the cross made after his departing parishioners and a backhanded slap on the snout for the worried malamute bitch when she started to leave her puppies to follow the Finn.

"Let's go," said Arkko Karvinin awkwardly. "I drive you, lady. Long way up there. Bad trail. Bad men. We get dogs quick."

And that was all the speech the squat Finn ever made about offering to drive a tenderfoot white girl forty miles into the teeth of a threatening, sixty-below, Bering Straits blizzard, to save a Sioux mad dog with a triple murder warrant hanging over his half-breed head.

XIX

Starr opened his eyes, staring blankly, his senses dragging back from beyond the edge of exhaustion. Feeling came first — the familiar feeling of Smoke's forefeet pawing at him. Then his ears cleared and he was conscious of the wolf dog whining and panting close above him. The realization of the third sense came with a heart-stopping jolt.

He was in a cave — gloomy, half-dark, shadowy, but a cave — every detail of its dry, rock walls and débris-littered floor was as clean as a calendar painting. Above him, also, each individual hair of Smoke's anxious face stood out as startlingly sharp as a settlement tintype. He could see! His eyes were back again!

The shock of it sent a hot wave of strength through him, melting the last of the murky veil shrouding his other senses. He came to his feet with a turning bound that left him crouched, facing the cave entrance, the joy of having his sight restored swept under by the sound that now set the short bristles at the nape of his neck straight on edge.

It came from outside and below the cave. Unless a man had spent his last twenty years in the Northland for nothing — unless his Sioux upbringing had been buried beyond recall by his contact with white civilization — his Oglala ears were recognizing that sound with hair-raising certainty. It was the crazy yammer of Indian dogs squalling along the last stretch of a strong-scent track line! There was only one thing for a man to do with those next five seconds. Grab up his Winchester and get out of that cave. Starr grabbed and got.

Outside, his newly returned sight worked as well as had his Indian ears inside. He dropped like a rump-shot caribou, rolled across the narrow ledge to the boulders lining the cave's valley edge, and peered down between them. His lean belly, flatly pressed to the naked rock, squeezed up inside him twistingly as a wrung sponge. Toiling up the granite spur 300 feet below was Tonga Nahahki and his five Chinik Huskies. Behind them, another 300 or 400 feet, came Angus McClennon and four of the men from the shack. Beyond them, down against the white snow of the Pushtash's floor, he could see

218

the two tethered sleds and their yelping teams.

His savage mind turned on his situation, slashing at it with the reflex anger of a trapped animal. There was no time and no place to run. They had him boxed up on that bare ridge. A greased weasel could not have squeezed out through the bouldered bars of that granite prison ledge without being seen and sight-run by those Chinik curs. And if the dogs missed him, their dead-pan master would not. He might get thirty yards into the open before the Indian could center him with his Spencer. After that, all you would find out was what the Chinik's favorite quartering-away shot was — snapped low and fast for the kidneys, playing it safe and just getting his game down, or held high and steady in the big coup gamble for the back of the head and getting it all done with one cartridge. A man did not have to waste any great time considering that choice. Not if he knew Indians the way Starr did.

No, a man had one way to go — McClennon's way. Straight down the slope. All his chips chunked in on the last jackpot. It was that, or lay on his shriveling belly right where he was and wait for them to come get him.

Murrah Starr was not a waiting man. He rolled back from the ledge rocks, hissed a warning to the wolf dog, slid swiftly down the narrow trail. Behind him, Smoke followed silent suit, belly down and crawling like a stalking lynx.

Shortly they came to a spot that lit the dark-blue fire in Starr's slant eyes. It was a place designed by nature for the ambushing needs of wolves, and of men who fought like wolves. The low growl of satisfaction that bared the half-breed's white teeth was blood cousin to the soundless snarl with which Smoke uncovered his yellowed fangs.

In a little cup of weathered detritus spread before them, a handful of stunted spruce had taken root. Just beyond their screening growth the trail dropped off steeply enough to make a man use both hands in climbing. In the few seconds after the Huskies had scrambled up over the lip of the drop-off and before they could come abreast of his spruce clump hiding place, Starr would have ample time to center his rifle on the spot where the Indian's head had to appear. The distance was not over thirty feet.

Very good, thought the half-breed. Tonga Nahahki was already dead. And away past time that he was. Starr had a moment to be thankful for the latter thought, as he cheeked the Winchester and swung its blued steel tube to bear carefully on the lip of the drop-off.

Yes, he had to make dead sure of the Chinik. Were it not for his presence with McClennon's posse, a man could have taken his sweet-stalking time, spent all winter playing Sioux cat and white mouse with the man from Nome. But with the Indian to track and trail for them, it made the game too dangerous — even for an old Oglala mouser like Murrah Starr. No, Tonga Nahahki had to get that first slug right where it would make him the only Chinik in north Alaska with a wide-open .44-caliber third eye squarely between the narrowed slits of the two he had been born with. And from the sudden scrabble of the Huskies' hard nails on the steep rock of the drop-off just below him now, Starr figured that his full-blood cousin was no more than ten seconds away from getting his Chinik eyes dotted for Sioux keeps.

But as with white mice and men, the best-laid plans of Oglala cats could go astray. In the first place the wind, moving lightly and constantly up the slope in its normal rising draft from the valley, fell away just as the first dog topped the drop-off. In the second place Tonga Nahahki's head did not appear where it should have.

Starr had only time to curse his stupidity in underestimating the Chinik's cunning, when the Husky pack leader cleared his nostrils with a suspicious *whoof!* and swung his blunt head toward the spruce clump. In the next breath Starr saw Tonga's head pop up over the ledge twenty feet to the left of the trail spot. While he was still holding that same breath, everything went to hell in a hand bucket.

The lead Husky started for the clump with a growling rush. Tonga's head disappeared back below the rise, safe inches ahead of the burst of snow and rock chips thrown up by Starr's snap shot. Smoke broke cover and sailed into the Indian dogs.

The big wolf's unexpected rush made no change in the plans of the Kotzebue pack. They were no settlement curs, no Nome culls, no alley-prowling cowards. Smoke was not the first wolf they had cornered, nor did they imagine he would be the last. The pack odds were five-to-one. There could be no doubt of the outcome. They closed on Smoke, carried him under by sheer weight of numbers.

Starr could not get a clean shot at them. The swirl and crazy, wild snarling of the five-dog fight moved too fast. He might hit

Smoke. That he would never risk. Clubbing his rifle, the half-breed waded in.

He broke the back of one of the two who had the wolf dog pinned down, and stunned the other one with a glancing head blow. Two more leaped to take their fallen friends' places, as Smoke found his feet. In the same instant the fifth dog went for Starr's throat.

The half-breed had no room, or time, to swing the rifle. Dropping it, he threw up both arms to protect his throat, went over backward from the jarring weight of sixty pounds of berserk Husky. As he fell, his hands closed on the brute's neck fur, just below his snapping jaws.

Smoke dived in under the first of the two dogs, coming for him. He slashed for a foreleg and found it. The bone broke like a matchstick. The stricken dog screamed and staggered free. The second Husky made the mistake of leaving the ground to leap for the wolf dog. Smoke rolled in under him, struck upward at his momentarily exposed belly. The wounded animal made no sound. He did not even know he was dead. He hit the ground, got back up, walked a dozen steps away before he tripped on his own entrails and went down.

By this time the dog that Starr had stunned with his rifle butt had recovered, was leaping to help his companion who had the half-breed down. Smoke whirled to go after him, but, as he did, the broken-legged dog drove back in on his three good limbs and sunk his fangs in the wolf dog's haunch. The latter ripped himself free before the grinding jaws could find and sever the great near tendon, hamstringing him. His own lightning-quick counter slash crushed the other's remaining, good foreleg, putting him down for keeps. With that, he was snarling to Starr's aid and it was all over in seconds.

He caught the second dog just as the latter seized the half-breed's arm, the tremendous vise of his wolf jaws closing on the back of the Husky's neck, just behind the ears. There was a single, snapping crunch. Then he flung the dying dog aside as contemptuously as he would have a back-broken hare. In the same moment Starr threw off the lifeless body of the dog he had strangled. When that was done, the only sound disturbing the dead quiet of the spruce slump was the scrape of the crippled dog's forechest across the rocky ground as he thrust himself toward the drop-off with his rear legs, his broken forelimbs dragging grotesquely beneath him.

Mercifully Starr shot him as he reached his goal. The short range smash of the bullet's impact carried him on over the edge, sending his slack body bounding down the slope toward McClennon's dumbstruck posse.

The whole action had taken less than sixty seconds. Only time enough for Tonga Nahahki to scramble back down the rocks to join them and warn McClennon in bobtailed Chinik to get away from there quickly. The wary Indian had already gotten on down the slope, but the big Scot and his white followers had only started to think about following him when the dead Husky's body came hurtling down upon them. That did it.

It was warning enough even for white men, not needing to be clarified by any Chinik-English translation from Angus McClennon. The last of the startled climbers had turned and started back down for the cover of the timbered flats below as Starr, bitter seconds too late, regained the cave ledge and the clear field of fire it gave him. He winged a couple of speeding shots after them. Just to let them know where he was — and where they were.

The big Scot had no need of the reminder. He knew where he was. He was six miles from the Pushtash diggings and his base of supplies, forty-six from Nome and any possible interference by Marshal LaMont or the Fort Michael military. Moreover, he was less than 300 yards from Murrah Starr and the $1,000,000 pot at the end of Angus Mc-Clennon's murderous rainbow.

XX

Starr crouched behind the cave mouth boulders, scanning the timber at the bottom of the slope, watching the movements of McClennon and his men. It was all he could do. The range was too great and too sharply angled downward to waste lead on. The only place he could see where he might get on up the sheer face of the cliff behind him, and so cross over the ridge, was a zigzag crack in the granite that started about 100 yards down the ledge trail. In the time it would take him to reach it and begin to inch his way up its narrow throat, they could easily get back up the lower slope to the spruce clump where he and Smoke had fought the Chinik's Huskies. From there they would have him under their rifles for the better part of an exposed 100-foot climb that he would need both hands to make. They would knock him off that wall like a crawling fly. While they were doing their knocking, his own Winchester would be slung across his back, about as handy and useful as a broken arm. No, they had him where he would keep. They knew it and a man could tell they knew it by their deliberate slowness.

Meanwhile, below the trapped man on the ledge, McClennon readied his siege. As Starr had surmised, he was in no hurry. He took his plodding, careful time in studying the terrain fronting the half-breed's prison, while patiently awaiting Tonga Nahahki's return from scouting the rear, east side of the ridge.

Above him, he could clearly see the cave opening yawning behind the ledge boulders. On the far, south side of the opening, the ledge petered out against the naked granite, offering no way up or down. On the near, north side up that ran the trail from the flats, and between that trail and the disappearance of the ledge on the south, the face of the ridge fell away in a plunging drop-off. It was a 300-yard, almost straightaway fall. It missed being vertical by just enough pitch to hold an unbroken pack of snow from ten feet below the ledge to the fringe of the flat timber. A mountain goat would think three times about trying that route — and then decide to look for another one.

Probing upward toward the half-breed's redoubt at a right angle to the main ridge, a secondary spur ran to within 150 feet of the ledge before breaking off and ending at an elevation some thirty feet below it. The twisting spine of this formation carried a bristle of spruce scrub to its very tip, making it easy for them to work along up it from the flats and be under cover every foot of the way. Once up there, they would have the ledge within dead-center range. After that, in clear weather like this, even in the relatively poor night light, the half-breed could not get twenty feet from the cave mouth without being seen. All that remained for McClennon to do, provided Tonga did not find any rear exit to the cave, was send a man back to camp for more food and blankets. Then just get comfortable and sit there till the half-breed starved to death.

Shortly the sullen Chinik returned. When he had made his report, McClennon knew that Murrah Starr was a dead man. There was no rear way out of the cave, no way down the back of the ridge. All there was on the other side of that gray granite wall was a sheer 600-foot drop.

Five minutes later, minus the man sent back to the diggings, the posse was ready to move up the side spur. But with Sandy

Macdonald posted on first-shift rifle guard opposite the cave ledge and with himself and the others gathered around a fine warming fire back in the spruce, waiting for the tea water to boil, McClennon and his siege plans got a nasty shaking up. The shaker was Tonga Nahahki.

The restless Chinik got up and left the fire without a word. He circled swiftly to get upwind of it, and was back before McClennon had time to figure he had gone to do anything more important than be polite about where he made his water in front of white men.

"Bad wind," he grunted uneasily. "Change too fast. Tonga smell snow."

"Snow!" McClennon was on his feet, saying it like it was a dirty word. "Ye sure, mon? There's no cloud in the sky. Ye must be wrong!"

"Him snow. You see."

"All right, when?"

"Kill-a-muck."

"How soon *kill-a-muck?*"

"Tonight. Him snow tonight. Big snow. Bad. Close trail quick. Two, all same three day. You see."

The other two men looked at McClennon, the threat of the storm as clear to them as to him. If it really came to snow, the half-breed would get away. Sam Pierce, oldest and least bold of the big Scot's followers, shook his head, shivered a little. "It'll be like grabbing for a diamondback rattler bare-handed and blindfolded," he grimaced, "trying to catch that 'breed coming off that ledge in a blizzard."

"Yeah, that's so," agreed Dave Reed. "If the Injun's right about that snow, we're whipped for this time. We might as well head on back right now. Once the snow's set in, there's no way we can stop him leaving that cave, and there's sure as hell no way we can get him out of it meanwhile."

"There's got to be a way to get him out of there meanwhile!" raged McClennon. "We've got him cornered. It might take us days to run him down again. We can't let him get away now. Think, mon, think!"

"I am thinking, McClennon," growled Pierce quickly. "I'm thinking Dave is right. There ain't no way we're going to get him out of there by tonight. Not short of blasting him out, by Christ there ain't!"

"Mon!" interrupted McClennon, heavy voice turning light and easy the way it did when his lethal mind seized on a pure inspiration, "ye've named it." He swung on Reed, the other man, black-browed grin letting out another murderous notch. "Aye, and was it not ye, Davie lad, that kicked open the 'breed's little powder house when we were looking around for a spare lamp last night?"

"Yeah," said Reed, not an imaginative man. "But I didn't find none."

"Aye." McClennon nodded happily. "And what was it ye did find, lad?"

"Not a damn' thing saving them two loose sticks of old DuPont in that busted case. Them and the half box of caps. What are you getting at?"

"Well, ye see lad, it's like Sam says," murmured the huge Scot. "We're a mite pressed for time just now."

Sam Pierce, at least, was back on the pace. "Gawd Almighty," he breathed, "you really are going to blast him out."

"Not out, Sam lad, in," corrected McClennon. "Providing Davie doesn't drag his feet about getting back up the creek before Burris starts back this way, we'll have Starr buried in that wolf hole long before Tonga's blizzard blows its first flake. Ye awake yet, mon?" He grinned at the gaping Reed.

The latter was awake. Within five minutes he was on his way, racing toward Blind Cañon with the remaining dog team and McClennon's orders on what to bring back — in addition to Big Tim Rafferty and the

Faro Kid.

On the cave ledge, Starr's squinting eyes narrowed as the second sled started back. The first team had left half an hour ago. Now this one. What did it mean? A man might figure that first sled. Likely it had gone back for supplies to set up a camp while they starved him out. But what about that second one? Why had it been sent? What was McClennon up to now? Well, one thing at least was as sure as Starr's parka was freezing to the ledge rock. On that last question a man did not have to guess to get his answer. All he had to do was wait for it.

For Murrah Starr that wait ended five hours later, when for the second time that day Smoke's warning growl awakened him. Satisfied that McClennon would do nothing until his men got back from the mine, he had crawled back into the cave, eaten a dry, cold meal, posted the wolf dog on guard, laid down to sleep. Sitting up quickly now, his first thought was for the time.

A glance out of the cave mouth told him that. The day had grown late. There was perhaps another hour before the long night set in. His nose, keen as any animal's, told him something else. The wind had come up and had switched northeast again. It was still clear outside but not intending to stay that way very long. That breeze had the salt smell of the sea in it, and the acrid, ozone tang of new snow lay in its freshening breath. There was another blizzard blowing in from the Bering Strait.

He had started for the ledgeside boulders to take a look around, when his instincts snapped shut on yet a third disturbing fact. Smoke had not growled because it was getting late, or because there was a change in weather coming. He was smart but not quite that smart. What was it, then, that he had seen or smelled, which Starr could not? In the foot-poised pause that followed the thought, the half-breed got his answer.

The wolf dog had seen nothing. Had smelled nothing. He had *heard* it. And Murrah Starr was hearing it now. A sound as familiar as his own breathing. Faint, muffled, metallic. Frighteningly remindful in its relentless deadly rhythm. The ringing, musical, *chink-a-chink* swing of a six-pound jackhammer driving a bull prod drill!

Starr's eyes swung to the roof of the cavern. It seemed impossible that the past twenty-four hours had not wrung his insides dry, but they had not. His lean stomach still had room to shrink, and proved it now as his hunted gaze fastened on the cave's ceiling just above the entrance. They were drifting up there! Putting in a set of dry holes with his own hammer!

The rest of it came to him with a sickening rush. Those two damned broken sticks of dynamite he had left in that old case from last summer's batch! The ones he had not wanted to use because the wax wrapper on both had worked loose at the crimp end, and to shoot them would be to risk a runny hole. Well, it was like the old Oglala saying: "Step over a buffalo chip, trip on a field mouse dropping." It was the little things in life that added up to big wailing in the lodges. Those two broken sticks of DuPont Superior were going to do for Murrah Starr what nine white men and a Chinik Indian had not been able to do. They were going to kill him. It was as simple as that.

He could wait inside the cave and be sealed in. He could creep out on the ledge under the overhang of shelf rock they were drilling into, and get buried there. It was just a question of how quick a man wanted to die. As to that, if he did not care to wait for the shots to go off, he could make a running break down the ledge trail right now. That way he would get it quicker yet — by Winchester — special delivery — shot across the short range of the ridge flanking his. A white man might have chosen the latter way. It was courageous, clean, highly charged with frontier dash and daring. But Starr was an Indian. He fought by instinct, not ideals. The last thing to enter his savage mind was to worry about whether or not his white enemies might admire the way he died. The Indian thought, always, was to survive. Their admiration went to the live runner away, not to the stiff-limbed, silent stayer behind. Slash and run was as much a credo with the Sioux as it was with the wolf brother from whom they had borrowed the strategy in the first place.

Hence, Starr stayed in the cave, his back to its cold wall, his wild intellect turning and twisting to find any last overlooked way a man might still have a chance to run for his life. But when, nearly an hour later, the drills quit chinking and he heard the dull *chunk-chunk* of the dynamite sticks being tamped home in the three-foot holes, he knew it was too late and that he would never run again. His tired mind had failed him. His slowing heart was bad within him. Mc-Clennon would have his way and the Push-tash mine would be his. Murrah Starr was going to die, right where he was. Safe in the back of the cave, waiting unafraid for them to seal him in. As old Sitting Bull had counseled him back in the boyhood years, there came a time for truth in everything — a time to fight — a time to run — a time to wait and pray. This was a time to wait and pray. Murrah Starr had fought and run as hard and as far as he was going to.

Looking outward to the tiny patch of darkening sky beyond the ledge, he began to repeat the Oglala Evening Prayer for little children. It was the only one he remembered, the one with which Tatanka had always tucked him into his sleeping furs.

Tunka sila le iyahpe ya yo,
Father, receive my poor offering,
Tunka sila canniyasa enpetuwi,
**Forgive me my failures as this sun
goes down,
Make me strong and unafraid when
the darkness comes,
Lift up my heart and lead my pony
with Thy sure hand,
For Thine eyes are become as mine
and I will follow You. . . .**

Starr never got to finish his prayer. There was a good reason. That Oglala proverb about the small mistakes being the ones that made the big miseries was not designed to work for Indians alone. It worked for white men quite as well. And in Angus McClennon's gloating case, with a peculiarly poetic vengeance.

When the latter bellowingly interrupted the half-breed's pagan muttering, he made a real big coup mistake.

"Hi! Do ye hear me down there, Starr mon?" he taunted from the granite overhang above the cave. "Are ye saying yer heathen prayers now, lad? Aye, and ye'd best be. Ye've two fine drill holes full of DuPont and sawed-off fuses over yer black head. But I'm overcome with Christian charity at the last minute. It's long been a failing of mine, as ye know." There was a deliberate pause. Then wildly: "Ye'll have sixty seconds, ye redskin scut! It's more than ye gave us in the shack, yonder, ye murdering bastard. Damn yer dirty soul to hell, Murrah Starr! And give the divil my regards when ye get there."

The sound of the Scot's deep voice in that last angry minute did something to the silent half-breed. A very simple thing. It just reminded him of Angus McClennon and all that he owed to him. For the entire time of the Scot giant's rasping challenge he crouched staring fixedly at the roof of the overhang, his Indian memory traveling swiftly along the back trail of brutality over

238

which the huge owner of the mercantile had led him. He was, in those still-eyed seconds, once more writhing on the bloody floor of the Scot's store — lying in the freezing gutter mud of Front Street outside it — awakening in the clean-sheeted fragrance of Erin O'Farrell's cozy bunk — crouched with her in the warm firelight of the cave in Dry Gulch Cañon — suffering again the exquisite thrill of that fierce instant when those soft arms had reached instinctively to take him in, and the white girl's heart had been momentarily laid bare before him that last night in the little shack in Fishhead Alley.

With the final thought, and the closing sneer of McClennon's tirade, Starr was back on his feet. And he was not using the scant remainder of his sixty seconds finishing his prayer. He was using it to arm into his pack, sling his Winchester and snowshoes across his tensing back, and growl a warning to the wolf dog. With that, he was ready.

Outside, waiting behind a sheltering outcrop safely beyond the smoking drill hole on the overhang, McClennon and his men had only time to see the hunched figures of the half-breed and his timber wolf shadow burst out of the cave, leap across the ledge, hurl themselves outward and downward. The next moment they had disappeared from sight, falling twistingly toward the icy drop-off below. The startled posse stared mutely. Before they could move, or think to move, the entire overhang cave mouth and thirty feet of the fronting ledge dissolved in a splitting burst of orange flame and smoke-black rock dust.

XXI

It was nearing dusk as Arkko Karvinin geed his lead dog to the right, swung the team across the headwaters of the frozen Snake, hawed them hard left and to a snow-showering halt at the confluence of Push-tash Creek. Pointing southeast, up the granite-flanked course of the tributary stream, he nodded quietly to Erin. "Blind Cañon up there, I think. Four, maybe five mile. You follow creek, you find."

Erin was tired, and very sleepy. Even just sitting in a snug Kiwalik sled got to be drowsy work after six hours and thirty-five miles. But when Arkko Karvinin pointed up that lonely, boulder-strewn gorge and told her, in effect, that he had come as far as he was going and that she could get out and start snowshoeing the rest of the way alone, she woke up fast.

Five minutes of small-voiced questions left her right where she had been when the Finn

241

barked the halt to his panting lead dog, sitting in a stalled whalebone sled at the mouth of Pushtash Creek, with a long hour's uphill journey on foot ahead of her and less than fifteen minutes of fast-fading light left in which to get started. Further pleading with Karvenin only worked the same stubborn circle again. The Finn had his short neck bowed. He was sorry for her, he grunted awkwardly. Also, he would like to help the half-breed. He was a good man — very brave — and a foreigner like Arkko himself. But he had done all he could already. The lady could go on without danger. McClennon's posse would not do her any harm and would surely see that she got back to Nome sooner or later. After all, she was a woman, and a pretty one.

But Arkko Karvinin was a man, and a foreign-born claim holder as well. That shaggy-headed bear of a man, McClennon, that human bull they called Black Angus, he would like nothing better than to meet up with Arkko Karvinin all alone and forty miles from Marshal LaMont. No, the Finn was sorry again, but he did not want to meet McClennon. Not him, or any of his gold-hungry posse. Not today, not tomorrow, or the day after. He was going back now, but first he would leave a last word of warning on how she must travel.

She must stay off the creek ice, which looked so inviting and easy. It was too new, not yet to be trusted. She must keep to the high bank, looking out for deep, soft snow where the side gullies cut into the Pushtash. She could tell these bad places by the way the wind had scooped them out a little lower than the safe snow lying over hard ground.

Erin got out of the sled. Arkko helped her lace on the unfamiliar snowshoes, walked with her a little way to point out a place or two of bad snow, so that she would learn to recognize them along the trail. He had turned, leaving her standing there helplessly in the growing dark, and started back for the sled when the dull rolling thump and trailing growl of the distant explosion of the cave blast reverberated down the Pushtash from the upper valley.

As Erin flinched to the jump of her heart, he came back and stood beside her. He said nothing. Only stood there, head cocked, keen ears bent to catch and decode the far-off sound of falling rock and cascading ice that came now behind the first *karr-umphhing* boom of the explosion.

"What is it, Arkko?" she murmured fright-enedly. "A snowslide?"

"Yes," gruffed the Finn. "Big slide, lady." Then scowling quickly: "But dynamite first. Two, maybe three stick."

"No! Why on earth would anybody be dynamiting this time of year? The mines are all closed, aren't they?"

"They closed." Arkko paused, scowl darkening, his slow mind groping for the answer to the question of who might be using dynamite for what purpose along the Upper Pushtash in mid-October, with the thermometer dropping past forty below and the last of the gravel beds frozen in weeks ago. It was a bad question. Arkko was afraid he knew the answer to it, too. Knew who was using that dynamite. And why. It had to be McClennon. It could not be Murrah Starr. With the odds at ten-to-one against him, and with him running on snowshoes against two of the fastest dog teams in north Alaska, the dark-skinned owner of the Blind Cañon Mine would hardly be using his time to put down drill holes and wire up dynamite sets.

The stolid Finn kept thinking. He thought of McClennon and his nine men mercilessly hunting down the friendless half-breed. He thought of Murrah Starr all alone and running for his life. He thought of his own mine, and of what Starr's savage example had meant to him and all the other square heads like him, back in Nome. When he had thought of those simple, harsh things, Arkko Karvinin turned to the white-faced settlement girl at his side.

"You get back in sled, lady," he told her softly. "I take you up there."

It seemed to Starr as though he fell through the air a full minute. Actually his wild leap carried him ten feet out from the ledge and thirty feet down from it. He lit clear of the bare rock immediately below the cave, slammed with breath-bursting force onto the hard crust of the slope's snow pack. Fortunately the angle of the decline was steep enough that it broke his fall instead of his back. He bounced outward and downward, skittering and caroming off the frozen surface like a dislodged, down-plunging boulder. Behind him came Smoke, spinning battered head over flailing feet.

The stunned half-breed had time to realize that he had brought off the first part of an utter impossibility. Far from being dead, he was alive and not even badly hurt. Moreover, he was already a third of the way down the slope. There was now nothing between him and the unbelievable safety of the timber below but another 200 yards of life-saving snowslide.

McClennon's DuPont blast split the ledge away from the cliff above him, hurtling its tons of shattered granite downward. He heard the compressed rock burst of the dynamite charge, then the gaining roar of the avalanche released by it crashing down the slope behind him. He remembered feeling the smash of it as its gathered fist of snow and cliffside detritus drove in under him, lifting him up in front of it and washing him on ahead of it into the uprushing edge of the timber. And he remembered thinking that he would be crushed to death against the trees, and setting himself to meet the shock. Then, miraculously, he was past the first of the timber, sliding free and unhurt. The next moment the slowing avalanche thrust him to a wrenching stop in a cushioning clump of resilient young spruce.

In the same dying surge, the slide spat Smoke safely out of its spreading fan, depositing him not a dozen feet from his amazed master. The wolf dog scrambled to his feet, nothing save his monumental wolf's dignity injured in the 900-foot fall. It was when Starr grinned him a grim welcome in Sioux and moved to imitate his lead by getting to his own feet, that he first realized he himself had not been so lucky. His bad left leg, the one that had never mended right after being shattered by that cavalry bullet years ago was pinned between two spruce saplings by a tub-sized boulder. And it was pinned sickeningly solid. It took him five minutes of white-faced pulling and kicking to work it free.

At first he thought it was broken again. But upon trying it, he found that it would bear his weight. It was the ankle, not the leg, if that was any relief. It meant that he would have to move and keep moving, or it would swell tightly and set up on him and he would still end up waiting helplessly on his belly for McClennon to come and finish him off.

He got into his snowshoes, anxious eyes scanning the ridge above as he struggled with the frozen fastenings. What he saw up there only set his stiff fingers to fumbling worse than ever. McClennon and his followers had left the upper crest, working their way along its windy spine past the powder-blasted stump of the overhang to reach the still intact ledge trail north of it. They were now halfway down that trail, less than a quarter mile from him, Tonga Nahahki far in the lead.

Starr cursed, unslung the Winchester, stumbled toward the edge of the timber to get a clear line of sight between himself and the Indian. That was better. One thing, at least, was going to be made certain sure as of right now. From here on they would be coming after him without the benefit of their Chinik tracking dog. He might have precious little time to delay but the ten seconds it would take him to center that slack-jawed son-of-a-sick-squaw would be worth ten miles of whatever trail was left to Murrah Starr.

The range was right, well under 200 hundred yards. The light, that peculiar translucent gloom of the early winter Arctic night, was close to perfect. The wind, falling off in the hush before the coming snow, was down to a dead still whisper. But the half-breed's second curse broke bitterly.

He could not pin his aim! The terrible beating of his fall had left him trembling like a wet dog. Even braced against a four-inch sapling, the waving barrel would not hold still. And the Chinik was dropping down the slope with the speed and rubber-ball bounce of a bighorn ram.

When he had let him come on another fifty yards, still without being able to catch him in the wobbling V-notch of the Winchester's rear sight, Starr knew there was not going to be any wailing in the Chinik lodges that night. A chance shot was out of the question. It would only tell them where he was, waste the life-saving minutes it would otherwise take them to search the avalanche for his body, or to scout its fanned-out perimeter for his escaping tracks.

He had one way to go now, southeast and as far southeast into the granite wilderness beyond the main ridge as the narrowing, upper course of the Pushtash would take him. If he could outdistance them, get into that crazy cut-up country where the eastern spurs of the Kigluiak Mountains locked into the western flanks of the Bendelebens — that vast bare rock and stunted spruce desolation that split the drainages of the Snake and the Fish — he might yet live to get his sights steadied on the Chinik, and maybe on one or two of his white friends. But whether he made it away by 500 yards or fifteen miles, there was now no choice left but to set out at once. With the third of the soundless curses, Starr fled back into the timber.

Moments later, Tonga Nahahki was prowling the empty edges of the avalanche. Behind him, nerve-strung, not talking, peering with him through the eerie gray night, moved Black Angus McClennon, and his six increasingly restless men. It was a tense twenty minutes before the Chinik came to a crouching halt on the south edge of the snowslide's crumpled fan: an even tenser thirty seconds as McClennon and the others clustered behind him to follow the sweep of his long arm and the guttural bark of his thick-tongued excitement.

Stretching cleanly away across the unbroken snow of the creek side, southeastward up the left bank of the Pushtash, lay a shuffling, double-printed line of snowshoe tracks. While the hulking Scot and his posse stared silently at the telltale sign, Tonga turned to the former with a final grunting burst of uncut Chinik. When he had concluded it, the Faro Kid stepped up to McClennon.

"What did the son-of-a-bitch say?" he gritted.

"The son-of-a-bitch," mimicked McClennon acidly, "said we're trailing hurt game. The 'breed's left shoe drags deep and twisted. He's either broken a leg or turned his ankle so bad he can't handle it."

"And what do you say?" asked the Nevadan, his dry voice as warningly sharp as the Scot's.

The big man looked at him. When he answered, there was the same dark wild look in his black eyes that the Kid remembered from that night back in Nome when the flood had cut them off from finishing Murrah Starr at the Snake River bridge.

"I say we're trailing a dead half-breed!" croaked Angus McClennon hoarsely, and turned and stumbled off through the Arctic twilight after the swift-gliding form of Tonga Nahahki.

XXII

As a boy in Finland, Arkko Karvinin had been reared on a bleak outland forest farm. His native land was a country as cold and harsh as the Pushtash. Arkko remembered its lessons well. He could track a Russian sable or Siberian fox across new glare ice. Or trail a walking ptarmigan over old hard-crust snow. Accordingly he found the half-breed's snowshoe sign at the slide's edge as quickly as had Tonga Nahahki before him. He also read as swiftly the grim story told by the overlaying sign of his pursuers.

Seven white men and an Indian, he told Erin, and two sleds with at least eighteen dogs. The man they were after was injured. He was dragging his left foot. The sign was very fresh, he went on. It had been made since they heard the blast, well within the past hour. As to the blast itself, the cliff above them told that story. Did the pretty lady see that cave up there? No, more to the left. There, that was it. Right there above that place where the ledge had been blown away. Well, that cave was what had been dynamited. It was what had started the snowslide. That was a certain fact. The guessing began when it came to saying why that cave had been blown up.

But here was one guess. Somebody had been in the cave, somebody else outside of it. Arkko would leave it to the lady to guess the rest, to guess who had been where. He would only ask her if she thought her friend, the half-breed, would have been trying to blast McClennon and his eight men out of any cave?

Between the Finn's bad English and broad pointing gestures, Erin got the point.

While it was sinking shiveringly into her, Arkko worked ahead from its brutal premise. There was a big snow coming, he told her. Maybe before another hour. Maybe not until midnight, or even after. It would be worse for the half-breed than for his pursuers. They had dogs, sleds, plenty of supplies. If they had not caught up to him before the storm struck, they had only to dig in and wait it out, knowing that no man could travel far against its merciless winds. Knowing, too, that when the blow abated and the snow stopped falling, their quarry's continuing tracks — should they continue at all — would be easier than ever to follow in the new, soft snow.

Arkko did not like to tell the lady the rest, but it was the truth and must be told. Her poor friend was as good as dead unless she could catch up with McClennon before the latter caught up with the half-breed. And before the blizzard caught up with all of them.

He did not add, nor did he need to for Erin's benefit, that he thought Starr was already better than dead, regardless. She could read that in the awkward, gentle way he reached out and patted her shoulder when he had finished.

It was a time for final questions. Erin had only one for the squat Finn. Would he still go on with her?

Arkko smelled the freshening northwest wind. He looked up at the scarred cliff, dug inside his parka, brought out a small flat can of Copenhagen snuff. Taking a sparing pinch, he rubbed part of it inside his lower lip, inhaled the rest of it with the lugubrious right and left side nostril sniff of the veteran user. After the lip-twitching pleasure of the sneeze had exploded, he muttered something grateful in Finnish, wiped his eyes, put the snuff can back, turned to Erin

O'Farrell.

"You get back in sled, lady. We go on." Then, shaking his blond beard and saying it to himself as he followed her toward the waiting dog team: "Not very far now, anyway. . . ."

Starr stayed to the left bank of the stream, where the going was fairly level and open. There was no question of eluding the posse now. It was a straightaway race. Either he beat his pursuers to the headwaters divide of the Pushtash, still a long mile ahead, or he did not.

If he could get into that granite gap up there where the climbing stream cut through the living rock of the Pushtash Portals, he could hold them off until the storm got started. The opening of the rock-choked crevice was no more than ten feet across. A single man could stand off a regiment all winter, or, anyway, as long as his ammunition lasted.

But Starr's twenty-minute, two-mile lead had shrunk dangerously in the past hour. Exactly how much he did not know, for he could only judge by the barking of the dog teams. With the wind shifting and cross-quartering the crazy way it was, that was not too sure a sign, either. But it was sure enough to tell him that his race for the upper rocks was going to be closer than a Mohawk haircut.

He forced himself to lengthen his crippled stride, his bad ankle grating audibly with every lurching step. Just ahead now, the stream dropped down a thirty-foot rock fall of half-frozen rapids. From the vantage point at the top of the falls he would have his last view of the trail behind him. Until he took that look, he would have no real idea how much ground the posse had closed since leaving the avalanche.

One thing was a tight-cinch guarantee. He would need at least a mile's lead to make the Portals. He prayed pantingly for it as he struggled up the last yards of the left bank's steep rise. Either he did not pray loud enough, or else his Oglala gods were not listening.

When he had wriggled across the crest on his stomach and twisted around to take his downstream look, Starr knew that as far as he was concerned the Pushtash Portals might as well be on the backside of the Alaska moon. McClennon and the main group, with the first sled, were less than 300 yards below him. The second sled, carrying the supplies and handled by Big Tim Rafferty and the Faro Kid, was only a snowball's throw behind the first. A long 100 yards in front of McClennon's straining team, Tonga Nahahki was halfway up the short climb of the rapids' trail. He was so close Starr could hear him muttering and grunting to himself as he scrambled upward.

The half-breed weighed his remaining chances with the last-minute detachment of the man who concedes he is already dead and needs only to be covered up. It was the damned dog sleds that were making the fatal difference now. If he could somehow get the men to leave them and come after him on foot, he might yet skin into the Portals ahead of them. But if they stayed with the dog teams, never. Between him and the upstream sanctuary of the Pushtash's narrow gorge, the going along the stream's left bank stretched, smooth and unbroken, the kind of ground a string of racing malamutes could eat up ten strides for his one.

All right, so the first step was to get them away from the sleds. That meant the cross-stream rocks, over yonder on the right bank. Over there, there was no trail at all. 100 malamutes could not have dragged a baby's toboggan forty feet into that tumble of eroded mother rock. They would have to leave the sleds on the left bank, cross the ice, and come after him on foot.

Starr figured it was worth one of his wolf grins, and gave it one. It was the kind of a chance the Oglala cynically called — *cetan mani ousta:* that of a lame hawk walking on foot. And while he was still grinning about it, Murrah Starr got up off his snow-caked stomach and took it.

The creek was wide and shallow at that point, backed up behind the head of the falls for several hundred feet, with an average width of some forty or fifty feet. The half-breed started across it, moving gingerly as a cat on a sagging sheet-metal roof. Smoke followed behind him, whimpering with apprehension.

Starr did not need the wolf dog's worried whines to tell him they were skating on something less than thick ice. That fresh sheet of glare freeze under them was thin and brittle as a store-bought soda cracker, as fragile as a streetwalker's morals and about as much to be trusted. Which was good and bad in the same breath. Where it might hold a man and a wolf, it would never hold 600 pounds of loaded sled and toenail-digging dog team. It would stop the sleds for sure, but it would also slow him and Smoke. You had to cross ice like that as though you were tight-roping over the main Yukon on a six-strand slack wire, without a balancing pole and packing eighty pounds of tame wolf on your back.

It would have been a different matter could they have crossed back at the head of the rock fall, where McClennon and his men would undoubtedly cross. There the water was shallower and the ice thicker. Back there a man, even if not a heavily loaded dog sled, could cross with relative ease. But he would be, if he were Murrah Starr, silhouetted, hard and sharp, for his pursuer's rifles, as he did so. Hence, for him and Smoke, it was either go across on the treacherous glare ice above the falls, or go across nowhere. They were within ten feet of the far side, when it happened.

Starr heard the popping creak of the hairline break a second before he saw its zigzag cracks fork out from under his feet and shatter like a hammer-struck window. He yelled at Smoke, threw himself flat, reached to catch himself on the thicker shore ice ahead.

He did not make it. His injured left leg plunged through to the full depth of the bankside shallows. Nor was that all. In stretching shoreward to save himself from going clear in, he had to drop the Winchester. Now, pulling himself onto the quaking shelf of the shore ice, he got to his knees, an anxious glance sweeping the ice behind him in search of the rifle.

It was gone, settled somewhere out of sight under less than two feet of crystal clear creek water! Yet it was as far out of Murrah Starr's reach as though it had been dropped off the edge of the Cape Espenberg ice pack. A crippled leg wet to the knee was bad enough. To plunge a perfectly good arm back into the water after the rifle would be suicide. If the temperature was one mark under zero, it was fifty or sixty.

No, the gun was gone. From here on it was Murrah Starr and his Sioux skinning knife against seven white men and a Chinik Indian. That wet leg, unless a man could run the ice out of it, would be frozen to the bone in fifteen minutes. These thoughts did not take three breaths to pass through the half-breed's mind. But in the time of those three breaths he was seeing something that snapped his decision to leave the rifle.

Tonga Nahahki had topped out at the head of the falls behind him. The Indian, bred, born, and cold-suckled to the icy breast of his native wasteland, read the deadly fact of Starr's breakthrough at a glance. He and the fallen half-breed stared at each other across the windswept ice for a full five seconds. Then Starr moved suddenly to come the rest of the way to his feet and the Chinik dived hurriedly back over the crest of the rise behind him.

The other's action surprised Starr, and twisted his dark lips with the second grin in as many minutes. Likely it was Sioux humor and would take a half-Indian to appreciate. But there it was all the same. With a crippled leg freezing up on him as he stood there and with his rifle at the bottom of Pushtash Creek and with nothing between them and him but twenty feet of thin ice, they were still afraid of him!

The thought of the lost rifle part of the Oglala joke straightened the half-breed's mouth. Of course! That was it! The damned Chinik had not realized the Winchester was gone. He and his white friends would think they still had an armed, fully dangerous man ahead of them. That fact, slim as its rotten thread was, might just hold them back long enough to let him try and run the circulation back into his numbing leg.

Kicking off his snowshoes, Starr threw them into the creekside brush, shouted in Sioux for Smoke to follow him, wheeled, and started to run. He was forced to keep to the slender strip of packed snow edging the little stream and footing the precipitous rocks beyond it. There was no other way he could get the straight-ahead, pounding speed necessary to drive back the lethal frost now creeping halfway to the knee of his ice-sheathed leg.

He was still in plain sight and in long rifle range when McClennon and the first sled's followers burst up over the rock fall's drop-off. The white posse at once broke out their guns and held up to throw a snap-shot barrage of long shots at the fugitive. As their arching lead began splashing the rocks and ripping into the ground snow around him, Starr threw a desperate glance over his shoulder.

In the moment of his hopeless look, they were already breaking off their long-range fire, leaving the sled and starting to run opposite him up the left bank. Tonga Nahahki, in their lead, was rapidly drawing abreast of him, would pass him in another minute and see that he had no rifle. Past that, there was no human chance of beating the fleet Chinik to the Portal narrows. The numbness in his left leg had spread upward to the knee, even as he ran. He was done and all done, and, if he could just get into that heavy stand of spruce in the rocks due ahead, he would have gone as far as he was ever going.

Seconds later, he flung himself in under the low-branched cover, lay panting and gasping in its sheltering fringe. He had only enough remaining to raise his dark head and stare helplessly out at the closing circle of his attackers.

XXIII

McClennon's posse was beginning to waver, as he led it back to the rock falls to cross the Pushtash at the greater safety of that point. When he ordered its hesitating members on across the few remaining yards of open creek ice above the drop-off with an unsteadily hoarse — "Come on, lads, we've got him now!" — not a man moved to follow him. He was five eager strides on his own way before he realized he was all alone.

It was enough to give even Black Angus McClennon thoughtful pause. He had nothing between him and the half-breed's waiting rifle but fifty yards of thin Alaska air. He took the nervous time needed to think that it was typical of the cold-blooded half-breed to lie over there in that spruce clump until that fifty yards narrowed to five. Then he added a couple of seconds to consider the fact that even Tonga Nahahki had stayed behind in the safety of the left-bank boulders. The last thought tore it for Black Angus. If the whip-skinny Chinik had turned suddenly Winchester-shy of the streambed situation, the wide-open middle of Pushtash Creek was no place for 300 pounds of white man to be standing.

He went for the left-bank rocks, head first, skidding the last few feet on his diving paunch. When he had rolled to a cursing crouch behind the protective boulders, Big Tim Rafferty led off pithily for the delegation from Nome.

"Sure now and yez ought to be happier than a scairt soldier findin' a handy latrine in the nick of time. Ye're that lucky. What ails yez, man? Keep up that crazy sweat ye're in to finish the 'breed, and yez'll be settlin' fer an ounce of Starr's lead instead of that cool million in creek dust back yonder." The Irishman shook his head scowlingly. "Jesus Murphy, McClennon! All in Christ's sweet name we've got to do is set over here on our broad beams and leave the bloody heathen freeze to death!"

The other members of the posse were quick to back Big Tim. By damn, Rafferty was right! Even McClennon ought to be able to see that. They all knew the half-breed had gotten wet. They all knew how cold it was. They all knew how long it took a man who had been in the water to freeze to death at sixty below. What was it? Twenty minutes? Half an hour? Maybe all of an hour, providing he had got only partly wet? What the hell difference was it to them, anyway? Why not rustle up some wood, start a fire, and set it out in style? They had all winter. The half-breed had sixty minutes.

It was a logical, if long-winded, argument. McClennon bought it with that quirky way he had of shifting suddenly from ugly Celtic excitement to uncertain grizzly bear good humor.

"Aye, lads, ye've touched me deep. I'm a man of peace at heart myself. We'll boil a tin of tea just as ye say. Maybe one of ye will want to fetch a cup across to our friend yonder, as well."

"Faith, now," muttered Big Tim, somehow no longer in the mood either for good Irish or bad Scot wit, "and by the time yez ever git it boiled, I'm thinkin' the poor lad will not be after drinking any."

The Faro Kid looked at his raw-boned trail mate. The Nevadan had not opened his mouth since leaving the snowslide an hour ago. He did not intend any major speeches now. But when he had tacked on his bob-tailed Western amendment to Big Tim Rafferty's low-voiced motion of sympathy for

266

Murrah Starr, it left the posse meeting deadly quiet.

"Don't bet on it," was all he said.

Across the Pushtash, Starr stumbled to his feet, not able to believe what his frost-lashed eyes were telling him. They were building a fire over there! They were not coming on over after him. They were going to dig in and wait for nature to finish what they had started and now lacked the last-minute guts to go through with. Well, all right. Let them wait. He, Starr, would not.

As long as he could move a cramping toe or lift a cold-numbed finger, he was going to go on. They had had their chance to let him die decently, back in the cave. Now he would fight them as far as he could drag himself. How far that might be would not depend on them or on the weather, but on Murrah Starr — and on how far he could go to get out of the trap they thought they had him in.

He looked at his frozen leg, picked up a club-thick tree limb. Struck with grunting force at the leg, once, twice, three times. There was no feeling. It was as though he were beating a saw-log stump.

He nodded slowly. Dropping the limb, he swung around and studied the rising smoke of the fire behind the cross-stream boulders. With the second unhurried nod, his decision was made. When you were in a trap, caught and held there by a crippled, useless leg, there was one way out — the wolf's way.

He seized a nearby snag of dead-and-down timber, used an old north woods trick to shatter its brittle-frozen wood against a jutting boulder. With the dry, punky, rotten pieces he built a small, hot fire. When it was sucking into a steady spark-free flame, he opened his pack and got out his tea kit.

He made three cups, black and bitter as tanning acid, drank them down in smoking, mouth-burning gulps. With the last leaves drained, he put the tea things carefully back into the pack, began warming his hands over the dying coals. He flexed his fingers repeatedly and with attentive thoughtfulness. When he was satisfied with their suppleness, he stood up and drew his sheath knife.

He stood there for a long time, the haft of the knife balancing in his open palm, its channeled blade gleaming wickedly in the sinking firelight. Then he broke his eyes from the slim weapon, limped back over to the nearby boulder, his dark thumb repeatedly running the worn feather of its hollow-ground edge as he walked.

Moments later a strange sound carried

across the creekbed silence to McClennon and his waiting men. They broke off their uneasy small talk about the half-breed's being unfrozen enough to have built a fire, and listened intently. What they heard was the deliberate, slow, tooth-edging scrape of an eight-inch Sioux skinning knife being methodically whetted against a trailside hone of Pushtash granite.

Five minutes passed, then ten. The sound of Starr, sharpening his knife, had long since ceased. The ten minutes built into half an hour, crawled on toward the full hour. The utter stillness, continuing to stretch outward from the opposite bank, grew intolerable for the restless McClennon. Something had gone wrong over there. The half-breed's sixty minutes had ticked away without a sight or sound of further movement from him. That fact compounded with the strangely disturbing business of the knife and the even more disturbing realization that the first fat flakes of the overdue snowstorm had just begun to hiss into the fire made further waiting impossible.

The moody Scot's small eyes grew uglier. His chronic bad humor was in no way improved when, in response to his growl of concern over what the half-breed could possibly be doing that would call for a sharp knife followed by fifty minutes of nerve-wracking silence, the Faro Kid drawled: "Well, now, I reckon most likely he's fixing to shave." Nor was that laconic suggestion lightened any for McClennon when Big Tim at once took the negative to insist soberly: "If his blasted beard's as tough as the rest of him, yez could hear the scrapin' of it clean past Anvil Crick!"

Angus McClennon was buying no labored Irish grins or gunman-turned-gambler wisecracks. He whirled on the Kid, dark eyes blazing.

"God damn it! If ye want out, now's the time to cut yer yellow stick! I'll give ye just ten seconds, do ye hear?"

"Don't tempt me," said the Faro Kid, slouching to his feet and letting his hands drop to brush the butts of the Colts he wore cross-belted outside his parka. "I've about got a belly full of you and your Injun-varmint hound, McClennon." He detoured far enough to count Tonga into the fish-eyed final nod. "Let's get on with it."

McClennon had seen his hired gunman use those Colts. He had no idea of pressing for a personal demonstration just then — and never from the front. No, the Kid could wait. There were ways of getting behind his hardcase kind when they began to get too big for their britches.

"Sure, now, Reno," he made easy use of the Kid's seldom called Christian name, "there's no need for talk like that. Come or stay as ye like." He turned quietly to the others. "The same goes for all of ye. I'll only ask ye to remember that if ye stay here, yer cut of Starr's million stays with ye. If ye go, ye go without a dime. Make up yer minds."

"Ye'll be after crossin' over and jumpin' him now, is that it?" asked Big Tim Rafferty, slowly calling the last raise on the pay-off pot for his hesitant fellow gamblers.

"Ye've asked a question," replied McClennon carefully, "I'll answer ye with one. What would ye do with a million sure dollars thirty seconds away?" He held up, letting it sink into them before shoving in his last stack of blues. "And," he concluded softly, "with a Bering Sea blizzard set to snow under yer last chance at it inside the hour?"

The men looked at one another, and again it was Big Tim who put the words to what they all were thinking. "Sure and the Kid's already said it," muttered the Irishman, crossing himself uneasily. "Let's git on with it."

With the ponderous deliberation that so oddly mismated with his treacherous temper made him the implacable murderer he was,

Black Angus McClennon got on with it. Ordering the nine dogs of the lead team unhooked and turned loose, he divided his men into two parties to cross the creek and close on the half-breed's silent fire site from the east and west simultaneously. He and Tonga Nahahki took two men and the upstream, most dangerous jaw of the eight-man trap, moving swiftly on up the Push-tash to get across it where it narrowed sharply at the foot of the Portals' incline. The Faro Kid and Big Tim, with the other two men, dropped downstream and crossed below the rock falls.

Once safely established on Starr's side of the little stream, both groups moved in on the crippled fugitive's hiding place with the most peculiar caution. It was true that a full hour had passed since the half-breed had gone to cover. It was also an unquestionable fact, from the quick dying away of its thin smoke, that his small fire had gone out fifteen minutes after its lighting. The third certainty was that no creek-wet human being could sit still for forty-five minutes without a fire in weather like this and still be breathing. It followed that they would find the half-breed huddled, frozen to death beside his heatless fire spot. Whether or not they would find his tame wolf, standing faithful guard over him, made no difference. That would be a matter for the nine malamutes. The main thing was that Starr himself had to be dead, that any last remaining danger from him had frozen, frost-black, in the creeping cold of the last sub-zero hour they had waited him out across the creek.

Understanding all this, the Nome posse still closed in on Starr's spruce clump as though its dry-mouthed members had a wounded sow grizzly with three sucking cubs cornered in their pungent cover. But when, ten yards out and with no sign of either wolf or half-breed life stirring within, the crouching malamutes got a close, hot noseful of Smoke's rank scent and rushed the clump, the nerve-strung spell was broken.

McClennon and Tonga were first to reach the half-breed's fireside. They were still staring, awestruck, at its deserted emptiness and had made no move to break up the snarling fight the malamute pack had started over some miserable scrap of food left behind by the departed half-breed, when Rafferty and the Faro Kid led the others up.

The Kid's practiced eye took in the full story of Starr's flight long before it had sunk in on any of his companions. The lean Nevadan was no stranger to posses — from

273

either end of the rope. He had been in on many a manhunt before this one, had run men, and been run by them, too many times in his Stateside past not to be able to read at a glance the fire-smudged fine print of a hastily abandoned campsite. As he stood there reading the grim page of this one on the far, frozen banks of the Pushtash, the Faro Kid was for some unaccountable reason smiling contentedly.

He was still standing there, still grinning his hard-eyed pleasure over the half-breed's incredible escape — while not understanding the exact means of its accomplishment any more clearly than his open-mouthed fellows — when Tonga Nahahki broke the speechless circle to leap among the yammering malamutes with his clubbed rifle.

The aroused brutes were snarlingly reluctant to surrender whatever it was they were fighting over, and it was not until Big Tim and the Kid had jumped in to help the Chinik that they dropped it and slunk back, bloody-jawed. Tonga Nahahki looked down impassively. Big Tim's china-blue eyes bugged. The Faro Kid's chill glance swept to Angus McClennon.

"Come along up and have a look," he told him.

The big Scot stumbled forward, the others following him. They came to a gray-faced halt, staring sick-bellied at what they saw lying in the trampled snow. The only sound was the retching gag of one of the men as he vomited uncontrollably.

"God in heaven forgive me . . . ," breathed Big Tim Rafferty, and crossed himself three times.

It was a human leg, amputated at the knee.

XXIV

It was when they saw the leg that McClennon broke. He started to laugh and it was a sound worse than Starr's sharpening his knife or the slobbering of the malamutes over what he had used it on. The men drew away from him, moving quickly to side Rafferty and the Faro Kid. As quickly the Kid stepped clear of them, where he could watch McClennon and the Indian.

Tonga stayed with his master, waiting beside him wet-lipped, grinning and bobbing his head vacantly, as though he did not understand how to laugh but agreed with the crazed Scot that something very funny had happened. The Faro Kid shivered, and it was not from the sharpening cut of the wind.

The coldness inside him only deepened when McClennon came around to smile fixedly at his frightened posse. If the lunatic laugh had not done it, their first look at that wandering empty grin should have. He was stark, staring, slack-jawed crazy. Yet the voice that came out of that inhuman face was McClennon's. It was as familiarly deep and resonant as it had been when they had started across the creek five minutes before. The men hesitated, not knowing whether to believe their ears or their eyes.

"Well, come along, lads. The 'breed can't have got far without this." He kicked the shapeless thing on the ground, not noticing how the men shrank back from it as he did. "Aye, another few minutes and ye'll all be millionaires along with Angus McClennon." He broke off to nod happily at Dave Reed, rumbling out the orders as offhandly as though he were standing in the mercantile's back room. "Davie, ye and Sandy drop back down the crick to see he doesn't try doubling back around us in the timber. Tonga and me and the others will run his track straight on. Rafferty, ye and the Kid swing wide to. . . ."

Big Tim stepped forward, his three-day beard bristling angrily as a chestnut burr. "Rafferty ain't swingin' nowhere, McClennon. I'll not take another step after a lad with that kind of guts."

McClennon's pig eyes narrowed. He shoved his Winchester into the pit of the defiant Irishman's groin.

"I say ye will, Rafferty!"

"And I say ye're pure babblin' crazy, Mc-Clennon." The burly miner ignored the rifle, swung around to face the posse. "We'd best be goin' now, boys. We've just time to beat the snow back to town. That is, providin' we've sense enough to set out this same shameful minute."

The metal *clang* of McClennon's cocking rifle lever bit into the stillness. But before his thick finger could close on the trigger, the forgotten Faro Kid cut himself back into the deal. The very close blast of the heavy Colt burst like an underfoot charge of Du-Pont. The Winchester spun crazily out of McClennon's grasp, caromed off a tree into a snow bank.

The Kid spun the single-action's cylinder, blew the smoke through the barrel, poked out the empty with the ejector rod, thumbed in a fresh shell, drawled quietly: "Make your point with your mouth, McClennon. I'll handle the gun talk."

McClennon looked down at his stinging hands, glanced toward the fallen rifle. When he returned his gaze to the Kid, the furtive animal gleam of the calculating madman was in his deep-set eyes. "I'll repay ye for that, mon," he whispered. "Never ye fear."

"I won't," said the Faro Kid. Then, quieter still: "It's your move, Mister McClennon. Likely you'd best make it quick."

"Aye," nodded the other. "That I will. Well, lads, are ye coming . . . ?" He grinned emptily.

He was still looking at the silent posse, still smirking vacantly, still waiting for their suspended decision, when the dogs at the abandoned sled across the Pushtash began to bay excitedly. In the next second they were answered from downstream by the challenging yelps of a strange team.

"Now who in Christ's forsaken name kin that be?" wondered Big Tim half aloud.

"It might be LaMont," offered the Faro Kid acidly. "But five gets you seven, it ain't. Good luck don't run that simple in showdown poker."

A hushed minute later Arkko Karvinin's Nome Huskies were topping the rock falls rise.

Five minutes later, the wavering posse had heard Erin O'Farrell's white-faced story and were wavering no longer. To the man they had had it. The news of the Congressional refusal backed up by the Finn's cold-sobering report — picked up in Front Street as he and the girl had come through Nome

— that the Miners Association had just voted overwhelmingly to accept the government ruling and throw open the membership to all foreign-born claim owners brought them stumbling hastily into line with Big Tim Rafferty's earlier decision.

Black Angus McClennon's hole was, indeed, deep enough for all of them. It was away past time to leave him and get far back from the yawning edge of it. Without any remaining hesitation, the beaten posse got.

They crossed back over the Pushtash with Erin and Arkko, using the safe ice at the head of the falls, Rafferty leading the way, the confused malamutes of McClennon's unhooked team slinking after them. Angus McClennon was left alone with Tonga Nahahki, and one other still-eyed witness, the Faro Kid.

But the demented Scot did not even realize the Nevada gunman had stayed behind. He picked up his Winchester and turned to Tonga, and the little group moving across the frozen creek held up long enough to shiver once again at his senseless laugh.

"All right, Tonga, let's go! *Kill-a-muck!*"

"Kill-a-muck, kill-a-muck," parroted the loose-lipped brave, as he wheeled and swung into his trailing crouch along the piti-

ful one-footed print of Murrah Starr's crippled track.

The Kid let the Indian go a dozen gliding steps before he shot him through the base of the spine. He straightened up, stood a moment, then buckled slowly at the knees. He was dead when his dark face plunged forward and plowed to a soundless halt, buried in the broken snow of Starr's dragging trail.

"I like to see a good man get an even break," said the Faro Kid to Angus McClennon. "Two-to-one is Injun odds."

Back across the Pushtash, the rest of it tailed off quickly and quietly.

When the Nevada gunman stalked up to the Nome miners, Big Tim just looked at him and said: "The Injun."

It was not a question and the Faro Kid did not answer it. "Let's get out of here," was all he said.

"How about him?" Big Tim nodded. The Kid and all the rest of them followed the Irishman's eloquent head bob across the creek. 200 yards upstream, just coming out of the thinning timber, scrambling clumsily upward among the steepening rocks beyond it, the huge Scot's fur-clad figure seemed somehow, and suddenly, to have shrunk.

"I figure," said the Faro Kid thoughtfully, "that his chances are about as long as the half-breed's left leg."

"How about his sled and team?"

"We'll leave them. LaMont might ask questions. So we'll have answers."

"Last we seen of McClennon he'd parked his sled and set out after the 'breed afoot. Is that it?" asked Rafferty.

"Near as I can cut it." The Kid shrugged, straight-faced. "Have the boys whistle in the dogs. They'll hang around the sled, waiting for McClennon before they cut out and shift for themselves. I got to talk to the girl."

His talk with Erin was just as brief. He made it as gentle as he could, while still not watering it down any. Starr had taken off his own leg. He had maybe as much as an hour's start on McClennon. But there was only one way it could end for the half-breed. If it had not already ended for him. Had the Kid not been sure of that, he would have left McClennon over there with the Indian. The way it was, Starr would not live out the blizzard. McClennon might. Provided he got his mind back and hit for the sled ahead of the snow getting hip-deep. But the half-breed would be dead come daylight. All any of them could do for him now was to hope the cold got him before McClennon did.

Meanwhile, unless they all wanted to freeze the same as the poor one-legged devil, they had better be making long sled-runner tracks for Nome.

But Erin, even against Arkko Karvinin's broken-worded pleading, would not believe it. Starr could not be dead. There had to be a chance that he might still be alive. Until she knew, with her own eyes, that he was not, Erin O'Farrell was not going back to Nome.

They could easily have forced her to go, the Kid realized. But something in the desperate, quiet way the Irish girl looked at him when she denied Starr's death got to him. Maybe there was a chance he was still alive and might stay that way. And if there was, this handsome Irish lass and that brass-gutted half-breed deserved the longest odds a man could give them.

He turned away from her, talked earnestly with Big Tim and Arkko. The two miners nodded their agreement when he had finished.

Arkko and the Kid would take the Finn's sled and leave the girl at Starr's diggings. They had fixed up the supply shed, tight and warm, before McClennon had sent for them. There were plenty of supplies still there. She would be perfectly all right there until the blizzard blew over and they could send LaMont out to find the half-breed's body and convince her for keeps. Rafferty and the other miners would take the second sled and head for Nome straightaway. The Kid and the Finn would follow along as soon as they had set the girl up cozily in the shed.

After an awkward pause, Big Tim suddenly offered his hand to the surprised Arkko Karvinin. The Finn took it embarrassedly and the two shook hands vigorously. "Faith now and why not?" scowled the Irishman at the watchful Kid, as though some apology were necessary. "Ain't we both fella members of the same bloody lodge!"

The Faro Kid nodded. He looked at Big Tim, smiled fleetingly, reached gracefully for the big miner's calloused paw. "Shake hands with a stranger from Las Vegas," he said softly.

When their quick grips fell apart, the Nome posse's dark part in the manhunt for Murrah Starr was ended.

Shortly the last human sound faded away down the Pushtash, and there was only the sobbing wail of Angus McClennon's abandoned malamutes to argue with the building howl of the blizzard wind.

XXV

High up in the throat of the granite cleft that carried Pushtash Creek to its tortuous source, back braced against the closing rock, eyes scanning the sweep of the streambed below, Murrah Starr waited for his enemies. Or for that more merciful end that meanwhile crept numbingly upon him.

He had gone as far as human will would take him. The last, almost perpendicular ascent of the faint trail from the creek floor to the narrow ledge of the Portals' opening wings where he now crouched had spent him utterly. Nor was there any reason to go on. The only important thing remaining was to be alive when the posse crawled over the ledge.

He fought off the deadly drowsiness, beating his arms against his body, pounding his freezing face with the heels of his hands, talking to Smoke, to the heedless wind — anything to stay awake until they came for him. Twice in the first 100 yards from the spruce clump fire, he had fainted. Both times the insistent wolf dog had aroused him, had pawed and bitten and worried at him until he had staggered up and gone on. Then, miraculously, the congealing cold had begun to seal the stump, shutting off the loss of blood, saving him the last shred of strength and consciousness needed to finish the long climb.

Now, more remarkable yet, there was the feeling in the leg again. It was throbbing and pulsing with acute pain and he knew, from that, he had cut it safely above the dead white line of the frostbite. The knowledge twisted his compressed lips. The thought that came with it was as grim as the blank smile that reflected it. Would justice take a final ironic twist? Would the leg that McClennon had cost him prove in the end to be the price of his own life? A man could hope. And why not? The very fact that he was alive was a series of crude miracles. Why not one more? What was to prevent the luck of a dying half-breed lasting just enough longer to bring the hated face of Angus McClennon first above the Portals' ledge? *Nothing!* he prayed fervently. It would all depend on the long odds of a man's last minutes, and on the spreading fire of feeling in the stump of his amputated leg.

The leg did not fail him. The constant, tooth-setting pain of its returning circulation kept Starr awake far past any threshold of ordinary resistance to the paralyzing cold. He was still alert and in full control of his remaining faculties when he saw the solitary, toiling figure far below. He did not need the second, searching, still-faced look. But he took it, to be absolutely sure. When he had, he knew that the Sioux Great Spirit had not forgotten him. It was McClennon.

He forced himself up off the ground, inching his back upward along the bracing granite, supporting the stiff-bodied effort with thrusting shoves of the fork-limbed crutch he had whittled out before taking off his leg. When he was standing, he called softly to Smoke, lurched away from the look-out opening, hobbled back into the narrowing darkness of the cleft. There, behind an outcropping twist of the wall that would force the Scot to come to him through a space that would no more than pass his 300-pound bulk, he and the wolf dog made ready to welcome Angus McClennon.

The latter did not keep them waiting. Nor did the end come far behind him. It was all

287

over within two minutes after he crawled gruntingly over the edge of the dizzy drop-off rimming the Portals' mouth. Thirty seconds dragged by while he stood panting on the outer shelf to get his breath back and to let his angry, bear-small eyes unravel the snow-marked sign of Starr's retreat into the inner recess. Another half minute passed while he gathered himself and challenged the shadowy stillness beyond.

"Do ye hear me, Starr? It's me, McClennon. I know ye're in there, so ye may as well answer up. We've a little fight to finish. Remember? Aye, and we'll finish it alone. It's just me and yerself now. The others are gone. All gone!"

The wild laugh echoed crazily away up the cleft, died cacklingly in the rocks above.

"Listen, mon, do ye not hear it? There's naught up here but ourselves and the wind. Ye've no murdering dynamite here. No black shack to hide yer yellow-bellied rifle. No sneaking Finlander or soft-legged settlement slut to bring ye any dirty government reprieves. Do ye hear me in there? Make ready, Murrah Starr. It's for the last time. Angus McClennon is coming after ye!"

There was no answer from the crouching shadows. No sound at all between the Portals of the Pushtash save the keening of the wind and the crunch of the sealskin boots going forward through the crusted snow. McClennon had started past the crowding bulge of the outcrop, Winchester on cock and probing tensely ahead of him, when Smoke leaped for him.

The wolf dog's eighty pounds struck him chest-high, driving him back out onto the shelf, his fangs slashing for the protective arm the Scot threw up to guard his throat. It was the right arm. The one that held the Winchester. Its massive wrist bones snapped like breaking twigs under Smoke's closing jaws. The rifle flew out of the nerveless hand, skidded across the snow of the shelf, upended over the edge, and was gone.

McClennon did not see it go, for in the moment of its disappearance his huge left hand was closing like a vise on his attacker's neck ruff. He whirled the struggling wolf dog above his head as though he were a day-old nursing whelp, swung him head and shoulders first against the granite wall. Dropping the gray brute's senseless form, he spun around to find the fallen rifle.

Instead, he found the gaunt, crutch-supported ghost of Murrah Starr. In the latter's dark hand he saw the turning glitter of the skinning knife, knew that this time there was no willing circle of friendly white miners to kick the half-breed senseless and take his weapon away from him. But in those final seconds, with his rifle and his mind gone and with his right arm dangling useless, McClennon remained the total stranger to fear he had been all his brutal life. He eased away from the wall and came for Starr as confidently as though he were back in the mercantile with half the miners in Nome standing by to grab the crippled half-breed's knife the minute he flashed it. Six feet from his awkwardly crouching opponent, he made his move.

Leaping high in the air, he struck at Starr with his feet in the vicious French Canuck style of kick fighting taught in the logging camps of his Scot-Canadian youth. McClennon remembered his murderous lessons well. His boots slashed into Starr's face and neck, stunning the half-breed, smashing him back against the outcrop bulge. The impact with the wall kept him from falling but knocked the crutch from under his left arm and sent it toppling out of reach. McClennon had seized it before it hit the ground.

Helpless to leave the support of the rock behind him, Starr set himself to meet the last assault. The muttering Scot came straight in, driving the heavy crutch at the half-breed's unprotected head with every ounce of force in his great body. With his own last strength, Starr twisted forward off the wall, right arm snaked back and coiled for the strike.

He felt the crutch splinter and break across the bowed muscles of his back, felt, in the same bursting breath, a far softer, more satisfying deadly sensation — the suet-slick, hilt-deep slip of his skinning knife into the soft muscles of his enemy's underbelly.

McClennon staggered away, staring down at the protruding haft of the knife in slow, head-shaking disbelief. He was still staring at it, still shaking his head, when his lurching, rearward stumble carried him back over the rim of the drop-off.

Starr dragged himself to the edge in time to see the hurtling body strike a boulder far below, bound outward into space, and fall free for the last fifty yards to plunge through the sheet ice of the shallow pool where the Pushtash footed the Portals' climb.

He lay there a long time, looking downward. He only broke his eyes away when he heard Smoke stir and cry whimperingly behind him. The wolf dog had a badly sprained shoulder, a six-inch rock gash across his skull, but was otherwise whole and able to travel. They started immediately back down the blizzard-drifted trail. Eight miles away lay the Blind Cañon Mine and the wreckage of his lonely shack. With the snow deepening like it was, his leg gone, and his pack and snowshoes thrown away, he would never make it. But he had fought for it and won it. And such as it was, it was the only place that had brought him any happiness in the wandering years since he had left his people and come back to die in the deserted solitude of Sitting Bull's last camp. Now he knew only one thing. As long as life and strength remained, he would go on toward it. Let the north wind laugh. Let *Wasiya,* the Winter Giant, blow his frozen insides out. Let the thin ice of the Pushtash lay in treacherous wait for his first false lunge with the probing crutch. It made no difference now. Murrah Starr was going home.

It was two full hours later, nearing midnight and the end of his last ounce of blind will to go forward, when a quartering shift in the wind thinned the blizzard long enough for Starr to see where he was. Even in the dark and through the swirling flakes he knew that place. How could it be otherwise? Forty yards away, over and across that wind-cleaned sheet of glare ice, he had lost a rifle and left a leg. He was standing opposite the right bank spruce clump. Since creeping down over the Portals' cleft ledge, he had come less than a mile!

He stood there, slumping on the crutch, feeling the sink of it settle into him. Yet, somehow, when Smoke limped up to him, pausing only long enough to growl and beckon him on with a strangely urgent wolf whimper, he went forward again. He had not stumbled a dozen steps when the wind quartered again and Murrah Starr held up to stare in stunned disbelief through the lifted snowfall. 100 feet beyond where he would have given up and laid down to let the long sleep close his tired eyes stood a parked sled and the snow-drifted mounds of its sleeping dog team!

The next moment he had ordered Smoke back and away and was lurching forward to meet the welcoming yelps and grateful whines of McClennon's awakening malamutes. There was a bad ten seconds when they got his odor close up, but Murrah Starr had handled dogs all his life and these were very handsome sled dogs, far from home and glad for the smell of any man. He only called out to them and told them to be quiet and to come along.

And he never altered the thudding swing

of his crutch until he was up to the sled and could throw it away and pick the dog whip out of its handle bar socket and curl it over their grinning heads and laugh with them as he called the wheel team into place and began bending the frost out of their frozen trace leathers.

XXVI

At the Blind Cañon Mine's rough shed, the Faro Kid and Arkko Karvinin stayed only long enough to make sure Erin would be all right. They spent a little over an hour doing so, gathering and stacking a week's supply of stove wood from the scattered cords of Starr's winter pile, rigging up a prospector's stove from an empty kerosene can found in the powder house, chopping out and toting up a batch of clean creek ice to melt for water, and knocking together a crude bunk from some salvaged shack boards. Shortly before midnight they set out down the Pushtash.

It was Arkko's opinion that their best service to the settlement girl would be in seeing that Marshal LaMont got in to her as soon as possible. Toward this end, the Finn felt that he and Father Jacquet's experienced team would be urgently needed. There were very few sled dog strings in Nome, and even fewer drivers, who would care to buck a Bering Sea blizzard back up the Snake on eight hours' notice. There was no one at all, in Nome or any other part of north Alaska, who could run the unfamiliar trail as swiftly and surely as Arkko Karvinin and Jacquet's superb string of matched Kiwalik Huskies. All the hardy Finn and his ten wolf-cross brutes would require before starting back was a few hours' sleep and an Eskimo breakfast — two pounds, each, of uncooked *quak,* the raw-frozen caribou meat that was the sourdough's emergency mainstay in a land where wood was hard to find and fires far between.

For reasons of his own, the Faro Kid did not argue the decision. Coming through Nome, Arkko had picked up a rumor that the Coast Guard sloop would lay over for twenty-four hours to take back the federal prisoner LaMont was bringing up from Golovin Bay. If the Faro Kid could get back to town in time to wangle a ride south on the government boat, he would like the lay of his personal odds a considerable bit better. There was bound to be some later looking into by the U.S. Marshal's office of McClennon's little gamble to jump the halfbreed out of his Pushtash claim. When

296

Harry LaMont got back from picking up the stranded girl and looking for Starr's one-legged corpse, it was a 100-to-nothing bet that, as the murderous Scot's chief two-gun cook and dirty bottle washer, the Faro Kid would find Seattle's winter climate a sight more salubrious than Norton Sound's.

Thus it was that as the storm howled past twelve o'clock and on toward one, Erin waited alone in the creaking shed on the Pushtash. She could not sleep, or bring herself to eat. The feeling, so strong only three hours before, that Starr was alive and would somehow find his way back through the blizzard, began to grow less certain. By the time Arkko and the Kid had been gone an hour, her earlier faith had burned down to the cold-embered facts. Without fire or food, forced on into the open blast of the wind and snow by McClennon's crowding posse, without his pack or his snowshoes and dragging and pushing himself on up the ice-choked throat of the Pushtash with his two bare hands and single tortured leg, Murrah Starr could not stay long alive. Even had he been able to, by some tough heritage of half-breed vitality, there was still Mc-Clennon. The picture of the Scot giant's relentless hulk, plodding along Starr's crippled trail above the spruce clump, came back to Erin now with frightening finality

No, Starr was dead. Mercifully, she prayed, and without any more pain at the end. But dead nonetheless, and as forever gone from his greedy enemies as from the only woman he had ever loved. Yes, the hunted half-breed was with his mother's dark-skinned people now. He would not be coming back to her. Would never come again down the barren valley of the Push-tash to the snow-swept desolation of his Blind Cañon bonanza.

As the last thought struck Erin, its chill corollary swung her fearful glance to the buffeting planks of the shed door. If anyone came back down the Pushtash that night, it would Black Angus McClennon! And if he did come, it would be with full knowledge of her part in helping Starr. For the whole angry story, from the hour of her rescue of his broken body from Front Street's muddy gutter, through her supplying of the new gun and the food pack that had started him on his terrible vendetta of revenge, had tumbled out as she faced the hangdog posse in the spruce clump. It needed no additional terror of present aloneness to widen the Irish girl's eyes as they lingered on the quaking shed door.

She was still shrinking from the thought

when the wind slacked suddenly and she heard the harness jingle of dog traces and the halting scrape of sled runners in front of the shed. The next moment she had seized Arkko's rifle, thoughtfully left behind by the Finn to bolster her lonely wait, and shrank back into the building's darkest corner.

Nothing happened. The wind held quiet. The door did not move. There was only the restless whining and barking of the big Scot's malamutes to break the eerie stillness. Then, suddenly, there was another sound. One that stopped Erin's heart in mid-beat and shut off her startled breath at half gasp. It sent the pulse-racing blood of the impossible hope pounding through her. She heard a high, thin, quavering mournful sound, the most beautiful, sad, and lonesome, wonderful sound Erin O'Farrell had ever heard. The close-by, shivery howl of an Arctic timber wolf. Smoke! The wolf dog! The half-breed's gaunt and faithful gray-furred shadow! Where he would be, could Murrah Starr be far behind?

Erin did not wait to answer the wild excitement of her own question. She was through the door before the crouching malamutes had leapt up to challenge the sobbing cry from the ridge above. While they were still yammering their fierce reply, she was weeping over the motionless, snow-caked figure sitting, unconscious, in the sled behind them.

How she managed to get Starr into the shed, she never knew. And by the time she had cut away his frozen parka and gotten him into the warm blankets of the bunk, the hysteria had left her, collapsed and crying softly at his side. She remembered cradling his dark head passionately to her breast, crooning to him over and over and over again that she loved him. Then the belated relief of her own eighteen-hour exhaustion gathered her gratefully in. Her sleep was as deep and dreamless as that of the dark-faced man at her side, her breathing as steady and soft and undisturbed.

And in all the lonely frozen world of the Pushtash there was nothing but peace and contentment and a long still time of blessed rest for Murrah Starr and his chosen woman.

What could remain to be told beyond the magic of that beginning hour in the blizzard-lashed shed above the unbroken winter snows of Pushtash Creek? The faithful re-appearance, forty-eight hours later, of Arkko Karvinin, bringing in U.S. Marshal Harry

LaMont from Nome? The things they had to tell about, from town? The kindly federal officer's deliberately looking the other way while the Faro Kid talked his way aboard the *Nelly Forsythe* three hours before she took the last tide out ahead of the closing icepack? The Miners Association's straight-faced vote to let Big Tim Rafferty off with a five-dollar fine? And its unanimous resolution to replace him as head of the membership committee with a foreign-born, squarehead Finlander named Arkko Karvinin?

Well, yes, perhaps these pleasant things. And then, as well, for the last full measure of awkward fulfillment it meant to Starr, his final acceptance as an equal among the board-and-batten lodges of the white brothers' camp on the beach at Norton Sound. With that, there remained but one small, other thing.

The way that Marshal LaMont grinned at his nervous host when he pulled McClennon's murder warrant for the half-breed out of his hip-pocket and used it to light the fire in the kerosene-can stove. The same fire that Arkko Karvinin had laid with a twinkling Finn eye toward starting a sourdough's celebration supper of broiled caribou *quak* and tanner's-acid tea. But all these things happened later, and were of small account.

The only thing that ever really mattered to Murrah Starr was that he had found, at long and heart-deep last, that for which he had sought and hungered above all the gold that would ever glitter in Alaska's coarse-grained gravel. He had found a mate with whom to share the lonely fires and faraway nights, and with whom to listen, when the springtime came again, to the wild cry of the south wind sobbing in the spruce tops.

ABOUT THE AUTHOR

Henry Wilson Allen wrote under both the Clay Fisher and Will Henry bylines and was a five-time winner of the Spur Award from the Western Writers of America. He was born in Kansas City, Missouri. His early work was in short subject departments with various Hollywood studios, and he was working at M-G-M when his first Western novel, *No Survivors* (1950), was published. While numerous Western authors before Allen provided sympathetic and intelligent portraits of Indian characters, Allen from the start set out to characterize Indians in such a way as to make their viewpoints an integral part of his stories. Some of Allen's images of Indians are of the romantic variety, to be sure, but his theme often is the failure of the American frontier experience and the romance is used to treat his tragic themes with sympathy and humanity. On the whole, the Will Henry novels tend to be based more deeply in actual historical events, whereas in those titles he wrote as Clay Fisher he was more intent on a story filled with action that moves rapidly. However, this dichotomy can be misleading, since *MacKenna's Gold* (1963), a Will Henry Western about gold-seekers, reads much like one of the finest Clay Fisher titles, *The Tall Men* (1954). His novels, *Journey to Shiloh* (1960), *From Where the Sun Now Stands* (1960), *One More River To Cross* (1967), *Chiricahua* (1972), and *I, Tom Horn* (1975) in particular, remain imperishable classics of Western historical fiction. Over a dozen films have been made based on his work.

"I am but a solitary horseman of the plains, born a century too late and far away," Allen once wrote about himself. He felt out of joint with his time, and what alone may ultimately unify his work is the vividness of his imagination, the tremendous emotion with which he invested his characters and fashioned his Western stories. At his best, he wove an almost incomparable spell that involves a reader deeply in his narratives, informed always by his profound empathy for so many of the casualties of the historical process.